FIREBRAND

A Corporate Elements Mystery

MEGAN PRESTON MEYER

Entropy Cottage

This is a work of fiction. All of the characters, organizations, and events portrayed in this novel are either products of the author's imagination or are used fictitiously.

Firebrand: A Corporate Elements Mystery
© 2023 by Megan Preston Meyer
All rights reserved.

ISBN: 978-1-950927-77-7 (paperback)
ISBN: 978-1-950927-27-2 (ebook)

14 13 12 11 10 9 8 7 6 5 4 3 2 1
First Edition

Published by Entropy Cottage
an imprint of Preston Meyer Publishing

Chapter 1

She had already driven the perimeter of the industrial park twice, and there was no more time to be killed. She parked, flipped down the visor for a last-minute mirror check, and tried to smile. Her reflection looked terrified.

Can I really do this job? What if I'm not smart enough? What if I mess up?

Currant Keppler had graduated from the University of Minnesota's Full-Time MBA program two weeks before, and all that stood between her and her first real corporate position was this parking lot.

Bias for action, Currant told herself, pushing aside the abstract what-ifs and worries and focusing on the concrete. She flung open the door of her Honda, forcing herself out of the car, and strode purposefully toward her future.

It had been less than a week since Currant got the job offer, and oddly enough, she had been reading about Alpine Chalet Coffee Company when the call came in. She followed all of the companies that she targeted on LinkedIn, and that morning, a post featuring a stock photo of a confident woman with a coffee cup and a laptop had floated to the top of her feed.

> **Hey, #Freelancers! Whether it's a side hustle or your full-time gig, whether it's your debut novel, web design for a client, or the next must-have app... Whatever you're working on, Alpine Chalet Coffee Company has you covered.**
>
> **Tell us about your hustle using #AlpineOffice**

Currant clicked on the post and was taken to a press release detailing Alpine Chalet's plan to add laptop-friendly seating to all their coffeehouses. It also outlined an upcoming menu expansion; the made-fresh-daily pastries and warm breakfast items that Alpine Chalet currently offered would soon be complemented by lunch options.

`Alpine Chalet Coffee Company is not just the place for your morning pick-me-up. Stay energized all day with our savory sandwiches, hearty soups, and fresh salads.`

The next paragraph described a pitch contest in which entrepreneurs could compete to win seed money for their startups. She was skimming the application requirements (*A ten-minute multimedia business plan? What does that even mean?*) when her cell phone rang.

"Currant Keppler," she said.

"Hi, Currant, this is Stacey Plesko, Senior Director of Talent Acquisition at Alpine Chalet Coffee Company. How are you doing?"

"I'm doing well, Stacey, how are you?" Currant analyzed Stacey's tone. Was she bearing bad news or good tidings? Currant got up from her computer and started pacing.

"I'm doing great. Listen, Currant, I'm calling to let you know that we'd love to offer you a spot in the inaugural class of our LATTE Management Rotation Program."

Currant pumped her fist like an umpire calling an out and bounced up and down on the balls of her feet. *Yes!* She had really wanted this job—all the other ones she had applied for after finishing business school had seemed boring. Good, well-paying MBA jobs at respectable companies... but boring.

"That's excellent news, Stacey. I'm glad to hear that." Currant kept her voice even, modulated, betraying none of her excitement—just as she had learned in her Effective Negotiations seminar. *Never let them see you hungry.*

Currant's pacing had taken her over to the window; on autopilot, she parted the curtains and looked outside. Thunderheads were marching in from the west, and the trim craftsmen bungalow across the street gleamed against the pewter sky. Her neighbor was mowing his lawn, racing the rainclouds as he tamed the grass between the sidewalk and the street, but Currant barely registered it. *I'm getting a job!*

Stacey pattered on about the other LATTE program participants, the great mix of backgrounds, and how much Alpine Chalet Coffee Company was looking forward to having them all on board. "So much so that we're offering a signing bonus."

That brought Currant's attention back indoors.

"Altogether, the total remuneration for the LATTE Management Rotation Program would be…"

Currant had a minimum in mind; Stacey's number blew it out of the water. *Holy shit*, she thought. *This MBA is paying off already.*

"Any questions? Great. I'll send over the offer letter and contract right away—we're looking at a pretty tight turnaround. Your first day would be Monday."

They said goodbye, and Currant punched the red button on her cellphone three times to make sure it was truly hung up. Then she bounced around the room in a crazy, jazz-handed jig.

She, Currant Keppler, was going to be a businesswoman.

The relief was intense. The University of Minnesota's Carlson School of Management boasted a 94% post-graduation employment rate for its MBA alumni, and Currant had been terrified of remaining in the shameful 6%. At twenty-four, she was several years younger than the rest of her cohort and hyperaware of not having 'professional' experience, so she had worked hard, dived deep into corporate jargon, and graduated second in her class. *And now I never have to work in fast food again,* she thought. *At least not behind the counter.*

Currant woke her computer from its hibernation. The Alpine Chalet press release was still open in her browser, and the cheerful white edelweiss in the company's red-circle logo smiled up at her from her screen. Currant smiled back. *I just landed a spot in a Management*

Rotation Program at a company that does almost $400 million in annual revenue.

She clicked back to her LinkedIn profile, then clicked **Update**. A few seconds later, a notification went out to all 491 of her contacts:

`Congratulate Currant Keppler for starting a new position as LATTE Management Rotation Program Participant at Alpine Chalet Coffee Company.`

I need to go shopping. She had made it through business school with two suits and an H&M blazer, but this was the big leagues; business casual every day required depth of closet. Currant grabbed her purse and hurried down the apartment building's once-grand staircase, pushing through the heavy oak door into the late-May afternoon. The air smelled of fresh-cut grass and impending rain, and the clouds held the promise of a cool-down. It was hot out, and the humidity was unbearable.

Currant welcomed the storm.

Chapter 2

In the western Twin Cities suburb where Alpine Chalet Coffee Company had their headquarters, the storm had already started. Gavin Woodrow peered at the two marketers on the other side of his burnished birch desk. "So how do *you* think things are going?"

They sat silently, tautly, each one hoping the other one would answer.

Then one of them did, because one of them had to. "Um, things could be better, absolutely, but it's really hard to implement without strongly defined requirements," said the CMO.

"Of course. But dealing with ambiguity is part of the job, isn't it?" A bemused expression, softened with a hint of a smile; a look that said *Help me to understand*.

"Well, yeah," said the CMO, squinting against the minimalist desk lamp. The soft white LEDs gave off very little heat, and yet sweat was beading on his forehead. "But—"

"Look, I feel partly responsible here," Gavin continued. "I guess I thought you wouldn't *need* strongly defined requirements because you'd be able to assess the market conditions and the business needs on your own." His eyes were sadder now, disappointment with a hint of compassion, carefully calibrated to evoke remorse without triggering indignation. "I guess I thought you were ready."

The CMO shrank into the modern molded side chair. He looked over at his colleague, but the VP was not about to come to his rescue.

"I'm genuinely sorry that I haven't been able to provide more guidance—to both of you. As CEO, I just don't have the luxury of micro-management. But I *can* bring in someone who can offer the visionary leadership that the department needs. We'll get a job requisition out today—I'm sure we can get a transition leader in here quickly enough that we won't completely miss the opportunity."

Utter shame filled both marketers' faces, like children asked to explain why the goldfish they swore they would care for was floating belly-up on top of the bowl.

The VP spoke for the first time. "No, you don't need to do that. We can handle it."

"But you're *not* handling it—that's the problem." Gavin spoke sharply now, with far less compassion. "And it needs to be handled."

"Although..." Gavin went on, almost to himself. "I'm not sure we can afford a net FTE gain right now, and most of the tactical work could be handled by an agency. Maybe this isn't something that needs to be in-house at all."

Across the desk, the deer-in-the-headlights shock gave way to cornered-animal desperation. *I* cannot *lose this job*, both marketers thought. *I will never find another one at this level.*

Then Gavin brightened, straightened, flashed them a smile. "But we'll cross that bridge when we come to it. I'll have Talent Acquisition start looking this afternoon, but these things don't happen overnight. Who knows? Maybe you two can pull it together before we find the right candidate."

Two simultaneous sighs of relief. A glimmer of hope, albeit a small one. "We'll get it done," said the VP, and the CMO agreed.

Whatever it takes.

Chapter 3

Across town, the rain was just arriving. The first drops fell as Currant pulled into Rosedale Center, the closest suburban shopping mall to her Saint Paul apartment. She jogged toward the main entrance, ducking inside as the downpour began. The mall smelled cloyingly of body lotion, buttered pretzels, and disinfectant, and wasn't choked with shoppers. She set a course toward Macy's.

Halfway there, she diverted, drawn down a corridor by the edelweiss logo and the smell of fresh-brewed coffee. There were two Alpine Chalet Coffee Company locations in the mall, a kiosk in the main atrium, and this storefront. She took in the ambience: cold grey stone and warm golden pine, softened by red gingham and coarse grey wool. *What would you call this?* she wondered. *Swiss mountain chic?*

"Hi! What can I get you?" asked a barista, approaching the cash register from the back room. She wiped her hands on her gingham apron and pushed one braided blonde pigtail over her shoulder.

Currant's stomach rumbled, and she realized that she hadn't eaten lunch. *An Avalanccino sounds really good. Maybe a Matterhorn Mint Chip... or a Salted Caramel Ski Jump. The menu board contained the calorie count, though, so she defaulted to her normal order.* "I'll take a medium coffee in a large cup, please. To go."

"Sure. Did you want the Geneva Jolt Light Roast or the Davos Dark?"

Currant opted for light over dark, and then continued on her mission.

Shopping was always a bit of an ordeal. Currant was one of those women who needed to try everything on; her proportions, while generally pleasing, didn't always translate well into mass-market dress sizing. Today, for example, she shimmied into one size-12 dress and practically wolf-whistled. The dress clung to her curves seductively—and glazed over that extra bit of belly. She tossed her shoulder-length hair, wavy today because she hadn't bothered to blow-dry it, and practiced a few poses in the dressing room mirror.

She was definitely more aligned with the 1950s' version of Hollywood beauty standards than those of today. With her pale complexion, green eyes, and dark auburn hair, Currant thought she looked a little like an Irish Sofia Loren. That is, until she tried on the other dress that she had brought into the dressing room. It was also a size 12, and even from the same label, but this one had her looking less like an hourglass and more like an alarm clock.

After deciding on a few items and doing her best to appear unaffected when the cashier gave her the total, Currant headed back out into the mall. *Good start*, she thought, and steeled herself for another store.

Three hours and several hundred dollars later, Currant pulled to the curb in front of her apartment. She got out and hunched into the back seat for her purchases, determined to make it inside in a single trip. As she gathered all of the bags together, the first trickle of self-doubt crept in. *What if I can't handle a real job? All I've ever managed is a sandwich shop. Who am I kidding with all of these fancy clothes? I'm not a Calvin Klein career dress—I'm a poly-blend polo and visor.*

She shifted her shopping bags to one arm as she dug in her purse for her keys. The front door tended to stick, so she jiggled it a couple of times and hip-checked it open. She marched upstairs and into her apartment, dropping the bags on her bed. *Of course I can do this job*, she reassured herself, hanging a black skirted suit in her closet. *I have an MBA.* Currant pulled on a pair of sweatpants, flopped down on the couch, and opened up her laptop.

She had only updated her profile with her new job title a few hours earlier, but her notifications were full of well-wishers. She scrolled through the messages, noting with interest who had added their own words to the auto-generated "Congrats on the new role!" text. Her mouse stopped on one message in particular—Luke Kennedy, Founder/CEO at Regulr, had not only congratulated her, but added

```
sounds really exciting - would
love to hear all about it. want
to grab a drink?
```

Chapter 4

Grab a drink? With Luke Kennedy? Is this for real?

Luke Kennedy had been one of her MBA classmates, although his Marketing and Entrepreneurship courses hadn't overlapped much with her Supply Chain & Operations track. Currant didn't know him well, but she certainly knew *of* him.

He was the Matthew McConaughey of the Carlson School of Management—handsome and charming with a bit of a devil-may-care attitude. He was confident and gregarious, and aspired to be the next Elon Musk or Travis Kalanick, minus the scandals.

"No, not like Sergey Brin or Dorsey," he'd tell people. "I don't want to be responsible for building a behemoth. Something like Tesla or Uber, scalable but still making positive change—*that's* what I want."

During his two years in the MBA program, Luke had envisioned, researched, and discarded three different ideas for the Next Big Thing after they proved to be more difficult than he'd imagined. An unkind person would call Luke a quitter—he preferred the term 'agile'.

Currant stared at the screen. This really *was* real. Luke Kennedy was asking her out. She spent the next six minutes crafting her reply.

```
Hi, Luke.

Sure, a drink would be great!
When would work?

Currant

218.555.7725
```

Perfect, she thought. *Enthusiastic, but not desperate. Casual. Efficient.* She read it over one last time, and then, heart pounding, she clicked **Send**.

Currant closed the laptop and headed toward the bathroom. *A job offer, a successful shopping trip, and a drink with Luke Kennedy*, she thought, squirting toothpaste onto her toothbrush. *Not bad for a day's work.* Currant finished brushing her teeth and grinned proudly at her reflection.

Her last few days of freedom passed quickly, and she found herself on Sunday evening, pulling open the heavy door of a trendy Uptown bistro. She scanned the room, hoping Luke was already there. He wasn't, so she asked the uber-hip hostess for a table for two.

"You don't have a reservation? We usually book up three weeks in advance."

"Um…" said Currant, feeling plebian. *Of course you don't just walk into a place like this and expect a table—this isn't Applebee's.* The hostess stared at her with a mix of sympathy and condescension. Then Luke walked in, and the hostess stared at *him.*

His chambray shirt and chinos screamed 'Just stepped off my sailboat' and whispered 'TikTok casual partial-tuck tutorial.' Currant's eyes widened; he was even more handsome and roguish than she remembered.

His boat shoes squeaked slightly as he approached. "Hey, Currant," he said, touching her quickly on the small of her back. To the hostess, he said "Luke Kennedy. Eight o'clock," and flashed his big white smile.

The hostess smiled back, grabbed a couple of menus, and glanced at Currant—this time with far less sympathy. "Right this way."

"After you, Currant." He brushed the small of her back again as he guided her past him to follow the hostess. Currant focused on the spot where his fingers had been all the way to the table.

After they were seated, Luke turned his smile towards her and said, "Currant Keppler." The way he said her name, with such intensity, did nothing to lessen the tingle along her spine.

"Luke Kennedy," she returned. His sandy blonde hair shone in the golden bar light and his deep brown eyes were aglow.

"So how's everything been going since graduation? Congrats on the job at Alpine Chalet Coffee Company, by the way."

"Thanks—I'm pretty excited about it." *How's everything been going since graduation? I've done nothing for the last two weeks but watch*

26

Netflix and binge-read John Sandford novels. "And post-graduation life has been slower-paced, which is great, because now I'm refreshed, revitalized, and ready for a new challenge."

Luke had been busy working on his startup, he said, but still found time for fun. He was telling Currant about wakeboarding on Lake Minnetonka when a waiter with very tall hair asked what they wanted to drink.

"What do you have on tap?" asked Currant. The waiter patiently explained that they had over 60 local and craft beers available—plus a few more on the nitro tap—and that they were all listed on the Beer Selection list accessible from the QR code laminated to their table. Currant fumbled with her phone and the waiter turned toward Luke.

"Do you have Naniboujou Gin yet?"

The waiter looked uncertain. "No, I don't think we do."

"Are you sure?" Luke asked. "Can you check?"

As the waiter and his hair retreated, Luke turned back to Currant. "Naniboujou is my buddy's gin," he said conspiratorially. "He has a micro-distillery over in Northeast

Minneapolis, and he's just about to bring it to market. I'm helping him build Word-of-Mouth by ordering it everywhere I go, so when he approaches restaurateurs, they'll know their customers are already asking for it."

Wow. As a Supply Chain and Ops girl, she had always been a bit skeptical about the Marketing program, finding it somewhat fluffy. *That's actually pretty clever.*

The waiter came back, confirming the absence of Naniboujou Gin. Luke sighed. "Okay, then just give me whatever *you* think your best gin is. In a Negroni."

Currant glanced down at the beer list on her phone screen and ordered the first thing she recognized. "And I'd love a Schell's Dark."

Their drinks came, and Luke lifted his glass. "To life with an MBA," he said. "To Alpine Chalet Coffee Company and to Regulr." Currant clinked her glass against his.

"Regular? Is that your startup?"

"Regu-L-R," he said. "No A in the last syllable. You know how when you go to the same bar or restaurant over and over again, you get to be a regular? You know them, they know you, and they know what you drink. It's the type of place—"

"Where everybody knows your name?" Currant interjected, "Like in *Cheers*?"

Luke froze, taken aback to be interrupted mid-pitch.

Really, Currant? She reddened. *Cheers? You've never even seen it.*

He recovered quickly and launched right back into it. "It's the type of place where you walk in and they pour your drink before you even order it. But what if you want to try *new* bars and restaurants? What if you don't want to be locked down? We live in an experience economy, and you want to experience as much as possible. You don't want to settle for the same bar or restaurant every single night.

"Studies have shown that we respond neurologically to both novelty *and* comfort, so we at Regulr decided to bridge that gap. How can we make you *feel* like a regular, without actually having to be one?

"That's where Regulr comes in. It's a blockchain-enabled platform that stores your order, name, and drink preferences. When you walk into one of our partners—we call them

Guaranteed Greeting establishments—you pull up the app, select your preferred drink from up to ten saved Favorites, and snap a selfie. Your order, profile, and picture are transmitted securely to the restaurant's POS. The bartender gets a push notification, prepares your drink, checks out your selfie so she or he knows who you are, and then serves your drink with a 'Hey, Currant' and a smile. You get all the benefits of being a regular—in a place you've never been before."

Luke sat back in his chair and looked at her expectantly.

That sounds ridiculously unnecessary, Currant thought. "That sounds amazing," she said. "I love the way you couple efficiency and community. I can see this appealing not only to the consumer who wants to establish that bond, but also to the server who craves that connection with his or her clients."

Luke's eyes were shining, so Currant continued.

"I feel like this would work especially well at places that cater to transiting clientele, like hotel bars or even catered events. It's easy to build up a relationship with someone that you have repeated interactions with, but this enables connection during those one-off transactions, as well."

Did that even make sense? she thought.

Luke beamed at her.

"Exactly, Currant," he said. "*Exactly.*"

They had a second drink, and conversation flowed. "So what did you think about Reichart?" asked Luke, referring to the forty-something adjunct professor who spent every afternoon in the MBA Lounge, even though his only official teaching assignment was a half-day seminar called Building Professional Relationships.

"The Networking guy? He was weird. Plus, I *hate* networking."

"How can you hate networking?" asked Luke. "We're networking right now!"

Currant's heart fell. *Networking? Just networking?*

But then later, Luke mentioned that their 120-person graduating class had produced no fewer than three couples on their way to marriage. "Which makes sense," he remarked. "Opposites *don't* attract. I need someone as driven as I am." His eyes lingered on hers a beat longer than necessary, and Currant's heart lifted right back up, and then some.

"Wow, it got chilly," Currant murmured as they emerged from the bar. It was a beautiful Minnesota almost-summer night, but the crispness of spring hadn't quite lost its bite.

"Are you sure you're okay to drive?" Luke asked as they reached her car.

"Yeah, I'm fine." She turned to unlock the door.

Luke caught her by the shoulder, spun her back around, and kissed her. It was a long kiss, respectful but insistent, and Currant couldn't believe it was happening. Then his lips were gone and time started moving again.

"What was that?" Currant asked, "A breathalyzer?"

Ugh, she thought. *That was not as clever as I intended it to be.*

Before she could devolve into panic, Luke laughed. He kissed her again, said good night, and headed off across the parking lot. "Have a good first day at work tomorrow," he called, halfway to his car.

Despite the chill, Currant felt warm. She got in her Honda, rolled down the window, and let the cool night wind blow through her hair.

Chapter 5

Monday morning. *Here we go.* Currant had made it across the parking lot and stood at the entrance, shoulders back, manifesting fearlessness. The smoked glass door opened on to cold white granite, and she stepped inside as confidently as she could.

The receptionist looked up and smiled. "Welcome to Alpine Chalet Coffee Company! How can I help you?"

"Hi, I'm Currant Keppler. I'm here for the LATTE Program?"

"Hi, Currant! Of course. Onboarding is in Matterhorn—come with me."

The receptionist, Gwen Kendrick, if the nameplate on the desk could be trusted, was out from behind her computer and shaking

Currant's hand in a matter of seconds. She produced a temporary visitor's badge, and Currant clipped it dutifully to the pocket of her blazer. When she looked up again, Gwen was headed down one of the four hallways that extended off from the lobby like bamboo shoots, and Currant found herself scurrying after her.

Gwen Kendrick walked really fast. Currant had to concentrate to keep up with her long strides and constant chatter. "Keep that visitor badge on you at all times, but drop it off before you go home, because it's only good for one day. I'll get you another one tomorrow morning."

Currant nodded.

"I'll give you a little tour as we go. Each wing is laid out basically the same way. Here are the bathrooms; this is the kitchenette." The receptionist motioned to a fast-retreating mini-fridge, sink, and microwave.

"There are conference rooms throughout the building, and they're all named after Swiss things. This one here is called St. Bernard."

Currant caught a fleeting glimpse as they sped past; it looked like every other meeting room she had ever seen, except for the huge picture of a mountain dog on the back wall, complete with a barrel around its neck.

"Right up there is the HQ Coffee Bar." Gwen pointed. "One thing about working here—you'll never be under-caffeinated!"

They turned a corner and Gwen slowed suddenly; Currant stopped short so she didn't crash into her. A large conference room loomed ahead of them, spanning the entire width of the wing. Its walls were etched with a frosted-glass mountainscape, the words *Alpine Chalet Coffee Company* repeating to form a border about two feet off the ground. Above the peaks and below the border, the glass was transparent; Currant could see all but the torsos of the two people in the room.

"Here you go—Matterhorn," Gwen Kendrick said. "Have a great first day!" Currant turned to thank her, but she was already several yards away.

"Hi! Are you Jenna or Currant?"

A cheerful, wholesome-looking woman, barely out of her teens, was standing at the end of the long conference table. The mug in her hand had a faded Alpine Chalet Coffee Company logo on it, and Currant could smell its contents from across the room.

"I'm Currant," Currant said. She crossed the room and shook the young woman's hand. *She looks like an American Girl doll*, Currant thought. *The pioneer one.*

"Great! I'm Karina. I'm the LATTE Coordinator." She motioned to the other woman, wearing a navy skirted suit and very high heels. "This is Purnima, one of your colleagues." Purnima was also holding a coffee mug, but the paper tag hanging out of it indicated tea. Currant shook her hand, too.

Karina asked Currant what she wanted to drink. "We have brewed coffee over there," she said, motioning to the two large vacuum carafes on the sideboard, "but if you want an espresso drink, the Coffee Bar is right outside." Currant, still shell-shocked from being hurried down the hall and peppered with questions, opted for a mug of dark roast.

Karina looked skeptical. "Are you sure you don't want a latte? Or a cappuccino? It's really no problem."

Currant assured her she was sure. She filled a logoed mug, inhaling the steam, and then poured in half a dollop of half-and-half. She returned to the other side of the mahogany conference table and stood next to Purnima.

"So where are you from?" Currant asked. *Wait—can I say that?* After spending the last two years in a university environment, Currant was constantly worried about micro-aggressing someone.

"I just graduated from the Stanford Graduate School of Business," Purnima said in an accent that was much more California than Calcutta.

"Wow." Currant looked duly impressed. "Did you grow up in California?"

Purnima said that she had, in San Jose in fact, because both her parents were professors at Stanford. "...but that's not why I went there," she said, a bit defensively.

She continued on a monologue that sounded like the answer to "Tell me a little about yourself," and was describing her undergraduate internship with a non-profit that provided web design and marketing services to other non-profits when Gwen Kendrick returned with more people in her wake.

The new additions introduced themselves as Jenna and Xander, respectively. They were both from the University of Wisconsin-Madison, and both, after being questioned by Karina, wanted cappuccinos.

"Come with me to the Coffee Bar, then." Karina, Jenna, and Xander left the room.

"Actually, a vanilla soy latte sounds really good," said Purnima, following after them. Not wanting to be left alone, Currant went too, falling into line like one more little duckling as they filed out the door.

She caught up to Xander as they walked down the hall. He had carefully coiffed brown hair with frosted tips and was built like someone who would give good hugs. Currant introduced herself, then added, "So are you from Wisconsin?" *I really need a better line of conversation.*

"No," Xander said, with the hint of a sneer. "I'm from Seattle."

"Well, if you wanted to work for a coffee chain, you could have picked one closer to home," Currant said brightly.

Xander looked pained. "True, but I really admire what Alpine Chalet is doing in the market space. They have a more… *Midwestern* vibe." He paused for a second. "I feel like I can make a larger impact here, since it's only a regional player, than I could at a company that's already entrenched. Small pond, you know?"

Currant got the impression that he had tried out for the hometown team but hadn't made the cut.

The HQ Coffee Bar was an Alpine Chalet kiosk set up in miniature. A triple-head commercial espresso maker gleamed in one corner, and two tough-looking industrial blenders, primed and ready, sat next to a stainless-steel percolator. Canisters of candied walnuts, white chocolate chips, and chocolate-covered coffee beans lined the long counter. The bar was nestled under a gabled, gingerbread-trimmed roof; a mid-sized set of antlers was mounted proudly at its peak. False windows trimmed with red gingham curtains looked out onto photographs of idyllic cows in peaceful mountain meadows. *This is kitschier than the one at the mall*, Currant thought. *I like it.*

Karina walked over to a refrigerator hidden beneath the counter and pulled out two shining pitchers of milk. She pulled a few levers and twisted a few knobs, producing two cappuccinos in a matter of minutes while monitoring the temperature of the steaming soy milk.

"You sure know your way around an espresso machine," Jenna commented.

Karina shrugged. "I've worked at AlChal for three years." She pronounced it *al-shall*, and Currant filed the abbreviation away for future use. "I started as a member of the Cabin Crew while I was in college. After I graduated last year, I got a job here at Corporate."

"Interesting," Currant said. *Sounds familiar. I mean, she doesn't have an MBA, but...* "How did you find the progression from working in service operations to working in a more knowledge-based environment? And could I actually get a cappuccino, too?"

"It was fine," Karina answered. "I mean, people are people everywhere. Although sometimes it's nicer when you only have to deal with them for the time it takes to make a coffee drink." She handed Currant hers.

"I bet," said Jenna. "Are you our dedicated barista, then?"

"Nope," Karina said. "You're going to learn to do it yourself—at your In-Store Experience Day." She explained that every corporate employee, from IT Help Desk Technician to CEO, was required to go through barista training so that they knew what they were supporting. To keep in practice, employees had full and unfettered access to the Coffee Bar during the workday. "The quarter after we installed it," Karina said, "productivity rose 25%."

Gwen Kendrick reappeared and delivered Max from the Ohio State University and Sung-Min, one of Currant's classmates from the University of Minnesota. They both requested double espressos, which Karina had ready in the time it took for a round of handshakes. She handed Purnima her soy vanilla latte and ushered the group back into the conference room.

They settled around the mahogany table, basking in caffeine and the muted glow of the PowerPoint projected on the wall, and waited for the day to begin.

Chapter 6

They waited for almost half an hour.

Karina's boss arrived in a whirlwind of hairspray and jangling bracelets a few minutes before 10:00 and bustled to the front of the room. Karina handed over the wireless presentation remote like a relay baton.

"Good morning. I'm Stacey Plesko, Senior Director of Talent Acquisition here at Alpine Chalet Coffee Company," she began. Her hair was a sculpted wedge of blonde, caramel, and cherry red highlights, and she had a huge, toothy smile. "First of all, I want to offer you a great big 'Welcome'. We are so glad you're all here as the inaugural cohort of our LATTE Management Rotation Program!" She beamed. "Now, let's just jump right into our

Onboarding," she said. "We're running a little behind schedule."

With a tinkling of bracelets, Stacey raised the wireless remote and clicked it at the PowerPoint projected on the wall. The title slide broke in two, the halves pulling apart to reveal Alpine Chalet's red-and-white edelweiss logo. The words **Mission**, **Vision**, and **Values** were written underneath the logo in the company's signature font. Streaks of light from the green laser pointer attached to Stacey's presentation remote bounced merrily around the screen.

"You know what? Let's skip this part. You can find all of this information on our corporate intranet." Stacey clicked the remote several times; bullet points like *"To be the world's preferred meeting spot"* and *"Integrity"* flew in from the right like wasps. A final click brought a group of smiling, multicultural business professionals twirling into view, and the word **Introductions** flickered on beneath it.

"Great. Now, let's go around the room and get to know each other a little better. Like I said, I'm Stacey Plesko. I think you've also met Karina, my assistant."

Karina looked up from her laptop and nodded.

"I'm Jenna Davidson." Jenna jumped in before Stacey could even ask who wanted to go first. "I have an MBA in Brand and Product Management from the Wisconsin School of Business at the University of Wisconsin—Madison. I'm really excited for the opportunity to be here at Alpine Chalet Coffee Company, and I'm looking forward to new challenges." She leaned back in her chair and looked over at Xander.

"Xander Erling. I'm from Seattle…"

Currant already knew most of his story from their hallway conversation, so she studied Jenna surreptitiously instead of listening. With her long blonde hair and moss-green eyes, Jenna was girl-next-door gorgeous. She was effortlessly all-American, and seemed like she'd be as comfortable tossing a football as she was allocating marketing spend. Currant had read a Wharton study in her last semester on how beauty could be a liability in the business world; *Poor thing*, she thought, with genuine pity.

"...and I'm looking forward to new challenges," Xander finished.

Sung-Min was up next. "I'm Sung-Min," he said, with just a touch of accent. "I'm Korean, my MBA is in Finance, and I went to the University of Minnesota. I'm really excited for this opportunity, and I'm looking forward to free coffee."

Currant liked Sung-Min; he was laid-back, but smart and no-nonsense. Since the beginning of business school, he had been growing his hair out and now wore it in a small man-bun. Sung-Min had always worn tee shirts and skateboard shoes in their shared Financial Statements Analysis class, giving off a surfer vibe; today, in his slim-cut suit and crisp white shirt, he looked like a GQ model.

The round of introductions jumped to the other side of the table. Purnima reiterated everything she had told Currant earlier, plus some. Stacey finally interrupted her, saying, "We're so glad you could bring all of that experience to bear here at Alpine Chalet. Who's next? Max?"

"...and I'm looking forward to facing—and mastering—all the new challenges that this

Management Rotation Program will bring," Purnima added before ceding the floor.

"Hey, guys," Max said. He had dark hair and looked like a hockey player. "I'm originally from Michigan, went to Northwestern for undergrad, and then worked in investment banking for a couple of years. I went back for my MBA and studied Strategy, and now I'm here." He grinned. "I'm looking forward to the free coffee, too."

Then it was Currant's turn, and all eyes were focused on her. "I'm Currant Keppler," she said. Her thoughts raced. What was she looking forward to? *I'm excited to be done with MBA school. I'm excited to actually do something, not just read HBR cases and sit through lectures and attend mock networking events every other day. I'm excited to finally have a real job.*

"After two years of business school, I'm looking forward to converting my theoretical knowledge into action," she said. "I'm excited to add value to the company, to experience the unique dynamics of the organization, and to gain a deeper understanding into how the corporate world actually works."

"I'm sure you will, Currant," Stacey said, looking suddenly tired. "I'm sure you will."

"Let me congratulate you all again for being accepted into our LATTE Management Rotation Program," Stacey went on. "We had so many great candidates, but you all are the best of the best—the cream of the coffee, if you will." She paused for a few obligatory chuckles.

"But don't get too comfortable. Your past experience got you here, but now you need to prove yourselves." Her wide, toothy smile disappeared.

Then it returned. "Pop quiz: Who remembers what LATTE stands for?"

"Leadership and Top Talent Experience," said Sung-Min immediately. Currant was impressed at his recall.

Stacey gestured toward him with her laser-pointer hand; the little green dot bounced on his chest like a night-vision sniper's guide. "That's right, Sung-Min! You'll get to *experience* working with the best *leaders* here at AlChal..."

Stacey emphasized the key words. "And, hopefully, become *top talent* yourself!"

I will become top talent, Currant told herself. *No 'hopefully' about it.*

"Now, I'm sure you're all super excited to find out what your first rotation will be… but here at AlChal, we like to make things fun. We'll be doing a little Reveal Party later on this morning where each rotation manager will come in, introduce themselves briefly, and announce whom they'll be working with! Then you'll go to lunch and spend the rest of the afternoon with your team."

"The six of you will also be working together on a LATTE-specific initiative. It's high-profile, high-stakes, and high-impact." Stacey clicked; the next slide fell in from the top, bounced twice, and settled into a stock photo of a baseball diamond. "Have any of you heard about our Full-Day Dining Initiative?"

"Absolutely," Jenna answered. "We're expanding our menu offerings to help our guests stay energized all day, not just at breakfast." Currant was pretty sure that was a direct quote from the press release she had seen on LinkedIn the previous week.

Stacey smiled even wider. "Exactly."

Max, who was sitting next to Currant, leaned over and whispered, "I don't get why there's a baseball diamond on the slide."

"You're probably wondering why there's a baseball diamond on this slide," said Stacey. She clicked on the picture, and a tiny, tinny, recorded sound trickled out of the laptop's speakers. No one could hear it.

"Hmmm…" murmured Stacey. She minimized the slideshow and brought up the audio menu. She switched the output method to no avail, and tried sliding the volume button all the way to the top. She switched back to the PowerPoint and clicked on the picture of the baseball diamond. Nothing happened.

"I think you need to be in Presentation Mode before it works," Purnima prompted. "Push Shift-F5."

"Control-F5?" Stacey pushed the buttons and nothing happened.

"No, Shift-F5."

"*AND HERE'S THE PITCH!*" said the laptop in a max-volume baseball announcer's voice. Jenna, sitting closest to the computer, jumped.

"That's right," Stacey beamed, now back on script. "To complement our new menu and cement our position as an office alternative for founders and entrepreneurs, Alpine Chalet Coffee Company will hold a *pitch contest*, where the best startup idea will win $10,000!"

"You all will own this," she went on. "You're in charge of both the strategic and tactical decisions and will be fully responsible for the outcome. And it's a tight timeline. The contest is in two weeks, on the day the new menu goes live, and we've already received dozens of applications. You'll do a half-day planning session tomorrow, so bring your brainstorming!"

The baseball diamond imploded and bounced like a tumbleweed off the screen.

Chapter 7

"Let's pause here for a second," Stacey said. "Who needs more coffee?"

The answer, apparently, was everyone. Currant followed her colleagues back out to the Coffee Bar and asked Karina for another cappuccino.

Ten minutes later, mugs in hand, the LATTE participants trooped back into Matterhorn. An unfortunate-looking woman paced restlessly in the front of the room. She was dressed like a Zara model that Currant had seen on Instagram, with large round glasses and a loose flowered dress. The model had looked delicate and adorable, like a baby owl; this woman did not.

"You said 11:30, but when I got here, no one was here." The woman scowled at Karina, who rolled her eyes.

"We just went to get coffee, Andrea," she replied, with an unspoken *Chill the eff out* trailing into the silence.

Karina waited for a few moments until everyone was settled. "Okay, guys, are we ready to get started? This is Andrea from Ethics and Social Responsibility."

"Hello, *everyone*," Andrea said, stressing the last word and looking pointedly at Karina. Karina muttered something about 'guys' being an accepted neutral collective noun and put in a pair of earbuds.

Andrea clicked past the title slide of her presentation. A new slide filled the screen; it said only

Andrea Pleney, MA
Head of Ethics and Social Responsibility

"Like Karina said, I'm Andrea Pleney, MA, pronouns she/her/hers, and I'm here to talk to you about our culture of ethical integrity and corporate responsibility here at AlChal. But first, I want to welcome you. I'm really happy to see such a diverse group of people in our inaugural LATTE class." She smiled broadly at the group, although Currant noticed a slight downturn of her mouth when her eyes met Max's.

Andrea advanced to the next slide. It said, simply, **Obligations To**.

"Before we begin, let's talk about obligations. As a corporation, we have certain obligations. To whom do we owe these obligations?"

"Our shareholders," said all six recent MBA grads in unison.

"Wrong!" said Andrea. "Well, not wrong, but not entirely correct. To whom else?"

"Customers," Currant ventured. Xander added, "Employees," and Purnima chipped in with "Suppliers."

"Those are all good," Andrea said, "But you're still missing a few very important stakeholders." She clicked again, and a bulleted list appeared underneath **Obligations To**: *Society*, *Earth*, and *Future Generations*.

"As Head of Ethics and Social Responsibility, my role is to ensure that all of us here at AlChal are fulfilling our moral and ethical obligations to not only make a good cup of coffee for our customers, but to create a better world."

She spoke at length about fair-trade certification, mandatory supplier sustainability audits, and environmental consortia memberships. "...but societal change begins at our own front door. We are passionate about making Alpine Chalet Coffee Company a safe, supportive environment in which you can grow both professionally and emotionally. Sometimes, though, others may try to take those opportunities from you." Andrea looked from face to face.

"Technically, your manager is your first line of defense. But I understand that, given the power differential between a supervisor and employee, you may not feel comfortable bringing your whole self to a difficult conversation with someone who has complete control over your career progression."

Andrea clicked to the next slide. **Report a Violation** was written in red over a blurry screenshot of the Ethics and Social Responsibility's corporate intranet page.

"If you are *ever* discriminated against, bullied, or made uncomfortable in any way, if you witness someone else being marginalized, or if you become aware of an unethical practice within the company, we are here for you."

Andrea, discovering the laser pointer, aimed it at the screen. "Click on this link right here to report a violation. It's completely anonymous."

"No, it's not."

"What?"

"It's not anonymous," Max continued. "Anything we send via webform through the corporate intranet is going to have our UserID attached to it, right?"

Andrea glared at him with so much venom that a lesser man might have reported her for contributing to a hostile workplace.

Stacey had slipped back in the room during Andrea's presentation, and now returned to her position at the head of the conference table. She switched back to her PowerPoint and stood silently, grinning at each of them in turn, allowing the anticipation to build.

"So," she said finally, "are you ready to meet your Rotation Managers?"

I was born ready. Currant had been waiting for this moment since her first day at business school. Unlike with an MD or a JD, there was no official admittance to the corporate world, no proof that she had made it. It wasn't like those old jokes: "You know what they call the person who graduates last in their class from medical school? A doctor." "You know what they call the person who gets the lowest possible passing score on the bar exam? An attorney." *You know what you call the person who graduates at the top of her class with an MBA? Nothing, until she provides value to a business. And I'm about to become valuable.*

Stacey nodded toward the door. Two senior directors and four vice presidents filed in and lined up along the etched glass wall.

"These are some of our top leaders here at AlChal, and I am so excited that they have agreed to mentor you during your first LATTE rotations. I'm going to ask each one of them to come forward, introduce themselves and their team, and describe the project that one of you will be working on."

"After that..." Stacey clicked on a WordArt question mark on the slide, and a drumroll sound clip played. "...they'll announce the lucky winner!"

Stacey flipped ahead in the presentation and introduced Dale Ascona, Vice President of Retail Operations. A bearded, bespeckled man, about fifty, came forward. His lucky LATTE participant would be rolling out new training materials for the store employees because the expanded menu triggered additional food safety requirements.

"Ugh," whispered Purnima under her breath, "I *hate* training. I hope he doesn't pick me."

Xander raised his eyebrows appreciatively. "I'll take him."

Dale waited for the drumroll, and then called Max's name.

Next up was Lucy Fischer, Director of Business Intelligence, who had managed to claim the first IT rotation headcount "...even though we're not really part of IT. We support the business with key strategic decisions—we just happen to report up through the CTO." She seemed tough and smart, and Currant hoped to hear her name. No luck—that assignment went to Purnima.

Steve Marzotti, Director of Logistics, didn't waste time on drama; he called Jenna's name as soon as his slide came up. She laughed good-naturedly when he asked if she could drive a forklift, but stopped when she found out that he wasn't kidding. Jenna would be managing user acceptance testing for a new inventory management system, and if she wanted the users to accept *her*, she would have to learn the ropes in the warehouse.

Stacey seemed perplexed as she surveyed the remaining leaders, but clicked to the next slide and called up Eleanor Banks, Vice President of Controlling. Eleanor wore an unassuming raw-silk sheath dress with pointed-toe pumps and seamed stockings, and described new standards for asset depreciation in a husky, bedroom voice. "Sung-Min," Eleanor said, and he closed his eyes in silent thanks.

Stacey's brow furrowed. She whispered something to Karina, who quickly left the room. When she flipped forward to the next slide, *both* of the remaining women came forward. Maria Huerta and Pamela Manx, Co-VPs of Organizational Development, were co-sponsoring a redesign of the succession planning process.

There were two LATTE participants left, but only one project. Currant held her breath.

The drumroll played, and they called Xander's name in unison. He let out an audible sigh of relief.

My new boss doesn't want me.

Currant had never been picked last in gym class because the teachers had always assigned teams, so she was unfamiliar with the humiliation that she now felt. *Whoever they are, they must have seen my resume. They must have realized that I am little and an impostor and have no corporate experience. They don't want me.*

The pressure of the first day, of meeting new people and trying to impress them, had loosed all sorts of stress hormones into Currant's bloodstream. She knew, rationally, that this was not an indictment on her worth as an employee or a human being, but the entire room was staring at her—*With such pity! Because I am pitiful!*—and tears burned at her eyes.

"Well, Currant, I apologize that your manager isn't here, but let's see who you'll be working with anyway!" Stacey put on a big smile.

Currant took a breath. *Stop it, Currant, you're not twelve. You are a professional and an adult and fully in control.* "Sounds great, Stacey," she said, and her voice didn't crack.

Stacey revealed the next slide—Beck Baker, Chief Marketing Officer, would be mentoring Currant through the rollout of new creative assets aligned with the Full-Day Dining Initiative.

Currant's smile quivered for an instant when the last drumroll played, but it righted itself again.

Luckily, everyone was on a tight schedule. AlChal's top leaders and newest employees trotted off toward their business lunches, and Karina returned to the conference room.

"I just checked the Visual Identity corner, and didn't see Beck." She settled into the chair next to Currant and pulled her laptop over so they could both look at it. "I'm really sorry about this."

Karina typed 'Beck Baker' into the intra-office instant messenger. A purple bubble floated in the corner of his profile picture, indicating his status as Out of Office. Karina clicked on the bubble to read his auto-reply.

```
Hi, colleague! Thanks for your
email. I'm not feeling great,
so I won't be in the office
today, but reach out to Gianna
Platinum, VP Marketing Special
Projects (gianna.platinum@
alpinechalet.coffee) and she will
take care of you! Thanks, -B-
```

Karina typed Gianna's name into the instant messenger and found more purple—evidently, Gianna wasn't in either.

"Really?" muttered Karina. "All the *other* departments managed to do the one thing they were supposed to do in order to get three months of free labor…"

Karina closed her laptop. "Well," she said with exaggerated cheerfulness, "I guess you've got the rest of the day off."

Chapter 8

The midday sun was in full force when Currant escaped to her Honda. The steering wheel was too hot to grip, so she spun the air conditioning knob to the max and drove out of the parking lot with her knee. She went a few hundred yards, parked in the very back corner of the neighboring office's lot, and then the tears came.

Currant let herself cry. When she was done, she checked her mascara and pulled her phone out of her purse. Luke had texted her earlier that morning.

good luck at your 1st day!

And then

```
i had fun last night..do it
again sometiem?
```

Currant's spirits lifted; she hadn't been expecting to hear from him for at least another two days.

Should I...? Normally, Currant would never admit interest so soon after the first date, but *he* had texted *her*. With the morning's events swirling in her mind, she took a chance.

```
First day wasn't so great,
actually. What are you doing
right now? I could use a drink.
```

Her phone chimed almost immediately. She looked down and read

```
that doesnt sound good.
grumbells in 30?
```

Currant smiled and headed downtown.

Grumbell's Tavern wanted desperately to be a dive, but had never quite managed. The drinks were strong, but a tad too artisanal; the lighting was dim, but the neon didn't buzz.

It was barely 1:00 PM, but the bar was already busy. The Twins were playing an afternoon game a few blocks away, and day-drinkers in jerseys chatted with the normal, sadder, Monday afternoon crowd. Luke wasn't there yet, so Currant slid into an empty booth facing the door.

A tattooed waitress came over. "What can I get you, hon?"

"I'm waiting for someone." Then, on second thought, she added, "...but I'll take a Schell's Dark."

Currant's eyes had adjusted to the bar's dim interior, so she squinted when the door opened a few minutes later. Luke stood silhouetted against the bright afternoon light like a sun god. She waved him over.

"Sorry," Luke said, sliding into the booth facing her. He eyed her almost-empty pint glass. "Been here long?"

"No, no... About ten minutes."

The waitress started over; Luke caught her eye, pointed to Currant's glass, and held up two fingers.

Luke looked at Currant, his chiseled features softening with sympathy. "Tell me what happened." The waitress came over with two more beers, and Currant told Luke about her morning.

"That's super crappy. I'd never do anything like that to one of my employees," said Luke. "And I'm surprised. Gavin doesn't seem like the type to appoint someone so flakey to a position like CMO."

"You know Gavin Woodrow?" Currant asked.

"Well, I don't know him *well*, but we run into each other occasionally. At TEDx Talks and stuff."

"Cool, do you do TEDx Talks?" Currant asked.

"No, but Gavin does," Luke continued. "And I admire what he's done with the company. From four locations in a mid-size market to the second-most-popular breakfast fast-casual chain in the country? That takes talent." He took a sip of beer. "Especially with such terrible coffee."

"You don't like our coffee?" Currant developed loyalties quickly; even with half a day under her belt, the barb against AlChal felt like a stab to her soul.

"I have to confess, Currant, I admire Alpine Chalet's leadership, but I'm not a big fan of the stores themselves. The espresso always tastes burnt, which I guess doesn't matter if you pour a bunch of sugar and artificial flavoring into it. And that whole cabiny mountain theme? I don't know. It just seems so…" he paused, looking for the right word. "…basic."

"I wouldn't say *basic*." Currant tried to sound casual as she defended her new employer. "We're familiar. Comfortable. Unpretentious." She fidgeted with a coaster.

"It's just not my vibe," said Luke, flashing his dazzling smile. He took the coaster from Currant and twined his fingers into hers. "I guess we'll have to agree to disagree."

At that moment, Currant would have agreed to just about anything.

"If it makes you feel any better, I had a disappointing morning, too. I've been interviewing potential co-founders, and the most promising candidate just withdrew. He got an offer to jump in just before launch on a mindfulness app that gamifies not looking at your phone."

Currant frowned. "That sucks."

"Yeah, he told me that he really resonated with my vision, but he has a kid, so he had to go head-over-heart. DiToxi just got first-round funding."

She must have looked appropriately sympathetic, because he continued.

"I mean, I know being an entrepreneur involves uncertainty, and I wouldn't trade it for corporate wage slavery for a second—no offense..."

"None taken," Currant said.

"...but funding *is* a major stressor for startup founders like me."

'Corporate wage slave'? Is that what he thinks I am? Does he not respect me? Her face wanted to

crumple, but she fought it. *Well, he's not the only one. My boss doesn't even want to meet me.*

Through the fog of her introspection, she heard Luke pause; it was her turn to talk. *What did he just say? Something about stress?*

"You could try meditation," she said.

"Not a bad idea. Maybe I'll wait till after DiToxi launches and then download all of the *other* apps in the Mindfulness/Meditation category."

He took a sip of beer. "I believe so strongly in Regulr's mission, but there are a million startups out there competing for attention. I know that if I put Regulr up against any of the other companies on the scene right now, it would be no contest. But it's *such* a networking game these days—you have to know someone." Luke sighed. "I just wish we could get some visibility."

I wish I had less *visibility*, Currant thought. Her brain flashed back to the Matterhorn conference room and the sea of eyes staring up at her in pity. A fresh wave of visceral humiliation rolled over her, and she squeezed her eyes shut for a second until it ebbed.

"You know what I mean?" Luke prompted.

What does he mean about what? Currant, actively listen!

"Um, yeah… That *does* sound tough. But resilience is crucial to success, and you strike me as someone with grit. That's such an important characteristic."

Luke smiled, but not with his eyes.

Currant panicked. *Should I have been more compassionate?*

A few seconds of silence.

"So do you like baseball?" Luke asked.

"Yeah, I do." She brightened.

"The Twins are doing great this year," Luke said. "We have a really strong bullpen."

"That's a relief," said Currant. Luke didn't react.

She went on quickly. "I mean, I don't really follow the standings or anything, but I love going to games. I think it's the classiest professional sport—no brawls, no painted bellies, just a beer and a hot dog and three hours of leisurely entertainment. It's very dignified."

Luke nodded. "I know what you mean— it's a little lower-key. You can still carry on a conversation between *pitches*." His eyes darted to hers.

"Oh, hey," Currant remembered. "That's another thing from this morning. Our LATTE cohort has been tasked with a super high-impact project—implementing a pitch contest for startups."

"Oh, really?" Luke asked.

Currant told him what she knew so far. "We don't have the tactical details completely ironed out yet—we have our first planning session tomorrow—but the winner will get $10,000, plus a ton of visibility. You should apply!"

"Interesting." Luke said, tilting his head. "But I don't know. My developer is just starting on the prototype, so I'll need to be pretty hands-on for the next few days. I'm not sure how much bandwidth I'll have..."

"Okay, yeah. Without a prototype, you're probably not even ready—"

"...But it might be valuable to sit down and put some thoughts together. To craft the story, you know? Spending a few hours to pull together a ten-minute multimedia business plan could be worth it if it means that Regulr can start helping people form authentic connections even sooner. Loneliness is such a huge problem in our society."

Currant nodded. "Then you should *definitely* submit an application. The sooner you bring it to market, the sooner you start helping people connect."

"You know, Currant, you're right." Luke took a long swig, finishing his beer, and then thumped the glass down on the table. "I'll apply."

They left Grumbell's but lingered in the parking lot. The goodbye kiss turned into several, and when they finally pulled apart, Luke winked. "You seem a little more cheerful than you did when I got here." Currant was smitten.

She drove carefully, weighing the day. Distance, and the salve of Luke's charm, had eased the morning's humiliation. Tomorrow was a blank slate, a new opportunity to shape her future at Alpine Chalet Coffee Company; she would not waste it by feeling unworthy.

"Grit, Currant," she said out loud. "You've got to have *grit*. Resilience is crucial for success."

Chapter 9

"Good morning, Currant! Welcome back. Are you ready for Day Two?"

Currant's legs trembled in her kitten heels, but she matched Gwen's smile. "I sure am, Gwen. Thanks!"

"I saw Beck walk by a couple of minutes ago, so at least he's here today! You know where your desk is, right? And do you want a latte?"

Currant confirmed that she knew where she was going and told her that she would grab a mug of brewed coffee on her own.

"Okay, then. Have a good one!"

With Gwen's last sentence bouncing cheerily off the marble, Currant made her way toward Marketing. She smiled tentatively at a few people in the hallway, and then veered left past the kitchenette toward the cluster of cubicles that Karina had pointed out the day before.

A broad-backed man peered at his computer, hunched so far forward that his nose almost touched the monitor. He was wearing a blue checkered shirt and suspenders. Currant's intimidation vanished. *Is my boss a nerd?*

The industrial beige carpet muffled her footsteps, so he didn't hear her approach.

"Hi… Beck?"

He jumped, clutching at his heart, but then quickly regained his composure. "Currant! Hi!" He smiled hugely and warmly at her, and the intimidation returned.

Wow.

Beck Baker was not a nerd. The vibe he gave off was post-industrial Paul Bunyon; his navy plaid was Burberry, his dark denim was vintage, and his work boots were Red Wing and unscuffed. He had twinkling eyes and an immaculately sculpted beard, and the suspenders were ironic.

He stood up, right hand extended, left hand brushing at the hair sideswept rakishly over one eye. It was pomaded in place, so didn't move, and Currant thought she heard it crunch.

Her new boss was like the Brawny man for organic, reusable, bamboo-fiber towel alternatives. They shook hands, and Currant tried not to stare.

"Do you want a latte?" Beck asked.

Ten minutes later, Beck took a sip of his mocha. "It's a super exciting time to be in Visual Identity, Currant."

They were in a casual meeting area near their desks, carved off from the aisle like a double-wide cubicle, furnished with bold designer living room furniture and whiteboards. "PS, we call this the Marketini Lounge," Beck said, sinking into an armchair covered in screaming fuchsia velvet. "It's perfect for informal chats and spontaneous collaboration. Lower-key than a conference room, you know?"

"Absolutely," Currant said. She sat rigidly on a shamrock green love seat, coffee mug clamped in her hands.

"Anyway. Back to Viz Ident. With the Full-Day Dining Initiative, Currant, Alpine Chalet is making a major, major change. We're moving from a place to get your coffee in the morning to a place where you can fuel your *entire* workday, AM to PM."

Currant nodded. *Is it weird that I'm still holding my mug?* She pushed aside a stack of AdWeeks and set her latte down on the thick glass coffee table.

"Change is good," Beck continued. "I love change. But so many companies fail to implement change successfully, Currant. And do you know the number-one reason why?" He paused. "They don't tell the *customer* that they've changed."

Currant wasn't convinced that this was the 'number-one' reason, but she decided against asking for a citation.

"That makes sense," she said. "Most major strategic shifts are aimed at expanding the market to attract new customers. But we also need to emphasize our updated value proposition to our *existing* customer base so that we can potentially increase our share of wallet." She finished spitballing and watched for Beck's reaction.

"That is so true, Currant. Great callout."

Nice, thought Currant.

"But..." Beck continued.

Shit.

"But I'm not talking about announcing *operational* changes. I'm talking about communicating that *we've* changed. As an organization. At our core." He took a breath, then continued.

"Alpine Chalet Coffee Company started as a place where you could go to wake up, to bridge that gap between the sunrise serenity and the chaos of the workday. We were the last bastion of sanity where you could gird your strength before you went out and kicked some ass." Beck made a fist and shook it, lest the forcefulness of kicking ass be lost on Currant.

"But now, we are going to be more than that. We're going to *energize* you. Nourish you. Be there for you every step of your workday. We'll get you ready to kick ass, and then, when you're hungry from all that ass-kicking, we'll feed you lunch, wipe your brow, and send you back out there to kick even *more* ass!"

I should say something. What should I say? Currant smiled and nodded.

"*That's* the change I'm talking about, Currant. That's what we have to convey. A menu panel and a window cling can tell people that we have soup now… but we as the Visual Identity team are called to communicate to our customers that we are *here* for them. That we support them. That we are a nourishing, energizing, inspiring partner and that we help them to fit even *more* in their day. And you know how we do that, Currant?"

Currant didn't know.

"With all new Creative."

Chapter 10

Beck's phone buzzed, and he glanced at the notification. "Hold on a sec, I need to deal with this." He leaned forward, elbows on knees, thumbs pattering on the screen. "I *told* them not to use sans-serif," he muttered.

He put his phone face down on the fuchsia chair arm and turned back to Currant. "So. Your project."

Currant perked up.

"We're in the process of perfecting the new brand assets for the Full-Day Dining Initiative, which will convey the energy and change that we spoke about earlier. The second they're finalized, we'll need to be proactive on—"

"Becky Boy, are you talking to our new little minion?"

The voice sang out from right behind the shamrock green couch. Currant jumped, then turned, and found herself staring up into the meticulously made-up face of a larger-than-life bombshell.

"I sure am, Gianna!" Beck replied. "Currant, this is Gianna Platinum, Vice President of Marketing Special Projects. You'll work closely with her, although you'll be reporting directly to me. Gianna, this is Currant Keppler." Currant stood to shake her new colleague's hand.

Gianna Platinum wore leopard-print ankle pants and a snug, black turtleneck; Currant wasn't sure whether the curves they hugged were authentic, but they were certainly pronounced. Her patent-leather stilettos, cat's-eye glasses, and long, sharp fingernails were all the same shade of crimson, and she smelled of something floral and expensive. She had large hands, more calloused than Currant expected, and a very strong grip.

"Currant—I like that. Like the berry, right? You're kind of round and ripe-looking yourself! Ooh, and now you're turning red, too!"

"Is that what I think it is?" Beck asked Gianna, motioning to the tablet she was carrying.

"It sure is, honey. I just showed Gavin, and he digs. You wanna see?"

Beck's eyes lit up like a little kid's, and he rubbed his hands together greedily. "Yes! Show me, show me, show me!"

Gianna dropped onto the shamrock green couch right next to Currant.

"This is perfect timing," Beck continued. "I was just telling Currant that the brand assets for the Full-Day Dining Initiative were in the process of being finalized."

"Oh, they're finalized, all right. Feast your hungry eyes upon the new Creative for the Lunch Launch!" Gianna typed a passcode into the tablet, and a full-color vector image filled the screen. "Am I good or am I good?"

The logo *was* good. An enamelware camping mug sat on a grate over a roaring fire, steam curling skyward over a snow-peaked, line-drawn mountain. The cheerful, speckled red of the enamelware blazed against the mountain's crisp, clear turquoise; the goldenrod campfire completed the bold, spirited palette. It was a minimalist design, almost iconized, but it crackled with nuance.

"Gianna, this is incredible. I can't even begin to describe how perfect this is." Beck beamed. "What do you think, Currant?"

She studied the vector file on the computer screen for a couple of beats, trying to gather her thoughts.

"I love it. It absolutely conveys the change that you were describing earlier, Beck. Whereas the current AlChal edelweiss logo is round and soothing, this is vibrant and angular. It's modern and clean and shows a willingness to grow."

Whoa, that sounded really good, she thought.

Beck beamed even brighter.

Currant glanced back at the design. "And, wow, look how the steam wafts off the coffee—I didn't even notice that earlier!"

"Yeah," Gianna said, failing to look humble. "It took me forever to get that right. I wanted it to *imply* an A and a C, but not spell it out, you know? And subtlety has never really been my thing..."

Currant marveled. "It *definitely* has those nourishing and motivating elements that we want to bring forth for the Full-Day Dining Initiative. The campfire says comfort, but the wisps move the eye upward, evoking vitality and energy."

"That is *such* a great interpretation, Currant," said Beck. "I couldn't agree more." Currant swelled with pride.

"This is really great work, Gianna," he continued. "Really."

"Did you expect anything less, Becky Boy?" She pushed herself off the couch using Currant's thigh for support and sauntered toward her desk.

Beck turned toward Currant. "You should sit down with Gianna for an intro, maybe tomorrow. She has *so* much experience in the Visual Identity space."

"Sure. I'll get that set up."

"Perfect. Now back to your project. You've seen the new Creative, and you love it, but now we need to make sure everyone *else* can see it and love it."

Currant nodded.

"The Full-Day Dining Initiative requires full-scale rebranding, and on a super-tight timeline. We're talking *all* of the in-store collateral—cups, napkins, menu-board panels… I don't even know what all we need. There's a ton of stuff; this is going to be a major roll-out."

"I can imagine."

"*You're* going to be leading that roll-out, Currant." Beck paused so that the responsibility could sink onto her shoulders. "You'll be in charge of procuring all of the marketing materials necessary for a smooth go-live."

So my job is to order stuff with a logo on it?

"Wow," she said.

"I know, but I have full faith in your ability to succeed independently. As CMO, I don't have the luxury of micro-management, but if you need mentorship or a sparring partner, just ping me. I care about my people."

Currant put on a grateful face.

"Also, quick note on security," Beck continued. "I want a total blackout until launch.

No distribution, no print—I don't want anyone to see it until *everyone* sees it. Got it?"

Currant nodded. "Of course."

"Awesome." Beck slapped his knees and stood. Currant started to stand, too.

"Oh, one more thing—super important."

Currant sat.

"Don't forget pens."

"What?"

"Customers walk away with pens all the time," Beck said. "And then they see our logo whenever they jot a note. Pens have some of the cheapest costs-per-impression out there. Order a ton of pens."

"Pens," Currant said. *I'm basically Office Depot.* "Got it."

Chapter 11

The air in Matterhorn smelled like cheddar. Currant put her laptop down at the same seat that she had sat in for Onboarding and joined Xander at the back of the room. He was examining the industrial toaster oven that took up one end of the conference table.

"What is this?" Currant asked.

Xander shrugged. "Karina was doing something with it when I got here, but she had to run to the test kitchen."

Jenna walked in and crinkled her nose, and then Purnima came in and did the same. Max and Sung-Min arrived together, laughing as they opened the door.

"Whoa," said Max, stopping short. "What is that thing? And what's that smell?"

Karina returned to find all six LATTE participants huddled around the machine. "You didn't think we would schedule a Pitch Contest Planning Session over lunch without feeding you, did you? You guys are getting a sneak peek at the new Lunch Launch menu." She set a green plastic crate filled with individually wrapped items on the table.

Sung-Min had been inspecting the long-handled aluminum paddle, and Karina plucked it from his hands. She unwrapped one of the packages to reveal a prefabricated sandwich and placed it, paper and all, on the paddle. Then she shoved it into the toaster oven and pushed a button.

The cheddar smell intensified, the oven dinged, and Karina pulled out a golden-brown morsel that looked almost edible.

"This one is Kale Cheddar Chutney. Who wants it? We've also got a Gruyere Bacon, Rye Roast Beef, and Vegan Falafelcado."

Snippets of conversation bounced through the room as the LATTE participants ate their lunch.

"It was great. My project sounds super impactful…"

"…so far, the culture seems really healthy."

"…I love them. They're both so *fierce*."

"Yeah," Max asked. "What's going on with your bosses, Xander? Why do you have two?"

Currant tuned in.

"They're job-sharing," Xander said. "They each work sixty percent so they can spend more time at home, and AlChal gets 1.2 FTEs' worth of Vice President each week."

"I love that. Work-life balance is *so* important," said Jenna.

"Agree. They both work Monday through Wednesday, which means that on Thursday and Friday, I have the opportunity to practice autonomy and to steer my own growth."

Purnima dabbed her mouth with her napkin and stood. "Let's get started." She walked purposefully to the whiteboard, stride stunted by four-inch heels, and plucked a marker out of the tray. She wrote **PITCH CONTEST** in large red letters spanning the top of the board and then stood off to one side. "I think the first thing we should do is decide on our goal."

"Our goal is to organize a pitch contest for startups," said Jenna, following her to the front of the room. "I think that's pretty clear." She grabbed a blue marker and took possession of the other half of the whiteboard. "But what's our *vision*? Sung-Min?"

Sung-Min had just opened a green glass bottle of sparkling water, and he stopped mid-pour. "Our vision. Great question." He put the bottle down. "Our vision is to identify and recognize promising entrepreneurial talent that... um... mirrors AlChal's values and brand promise." Satisfied, he filled his glass.

Jenna scribbled **ID/recog entrepraneurial talent – ACCC values/brand prom** in blue on the whiteboard. "Great. Thanks, Sung-Min."

She spelled 'entrepreneurial' wrong.

Max leaned imperceptibly toward Currant. "She spelled 'entrepreneurial' wrong."

Purnima jockeyed to regain control of the conversation. "Okay, so we've got the *What* and the *Why* figured out. How about the *How*?" She drew a scalloped starburst, labeled it '**How**', and added a couple of spokes radiating off in different directions. "We need to mindmap."

Jenna drew a harsh, horizontal line across her half of the board. "Let's think in terms of timeline. What are our milestones? What do we need to make this happen?"

"Well, if we want to choose a winner, we need to determine the judging criteria," Max said. "Are we looking for social good or commercial viability? Imagination or pragmatism? Do we reward long-term potential or short-term wins? To make it objective, we should decide on a set of evaluation factors and then figure out an objective scoring system based on them."

"Yeah, and we probably need to recruit some judges," said Currant.

"What I hear you saying is that we need to think about the judging and criteria." Purnima drew a bubble atop one of her spokes and labeled it **Judging+Criteria**. "What else?"

Xander spoke up. "The pitch contest is just one element of AlChal's commitment to supporting entrepreneurship and creativity, so we really need to design a holistic marketing plan that brings across the full scope of that commitment."

"Right," Currant said. "And since the pitch contest is so soon, we'll need to start communicating it right away, or no one will know about it."

Jenna cross-hatched her timeline and labeled it **mktg: design/execute comm plan**.

Come up with your own idea, Currant! You can't just piggyback on everyone else. "We should think a bit about what actually needs to happen to ensure a successful event. The contest exists to market the new menu, so we'll obviously need catering. How many people do we expect? Will we provide a full lunch or just samples? Do we need tables for people, or just chairs? There are some logistics to work out."

"Those are all great inputs, Currant," Jenna said, "but I really think we should keep it big-picture at this point."

Purnima wrote **Logistics** in red. Jenna glared at her.

"What's our budget?" asked Xander. No one spoke. Jenna wrote **Budget?** near her timeline and underlined it. "Sung-Min, as a takeaway, can you check on that? You're in Finance." He nodded.

"Okay, I think we have a good framework for what needs to happen," said Purnima. "The big buckets are Marketing, Judging, and Logistics. Who wants to take the lead on each bucket?"

"Let's split the responsibilities along functional lines," Xander said. "I can manage the Judging workstream, since I'm doing my Human Resources rotation, and Currant can take Marketing."

"Great idea," Purnima answered. She wrote Xander's name in red next to **Judging+Criteria**; Jenna wrote Currant's name in blue by **mktg**.

"Sung-Min can manage the budget, since he's already checking on it," said Purnima. Jenna wrote his name under **Budget?**

"And since you're in Logistics, Jenna, you can take care of the catering and stuff." Purnima wrote Jenna's name under **Logistics**.

Jenna's marker froze mid-air. "Catering?" she said, with a hint of distaste. "Then what are you going to do?"

"She can help Currant with Marketing," Xander interjected. "I think that's one of the major elements, and the one that needs the most attention."

Purnima nodded and added her name under Currant's. "Max? You're the only one left."

Jenna added his name to hers underneath **Logistics**.

Max shrugged. "Okay."

"Amazing." Purnima snapped a picture of the red and blue whiteboard and said she would circulate it after the meeting. "This was excellent, guys. I'm super impressed by how quickly we hammered this out."

"Yeah—really great effort," added Jenna, but she was drowned out by slamming laptops and scooting chairs.

When Currant got back to her desk, Beck's chair was empty, and Gianna was talking loudly at her laptop.

What should I be doing right now? Her To-Do list contained two items: 1) **Set up Intro with Gianna**; and 2) **Work on project**. Currant checked her email.

"Ciao! Bye! Ciao!" Gianna was blowing kisses at her screen; Currant assumed the video call had ended and walked over to schedule an introduction.

Gianna looked up at her, then very deliberately looked back down. She typed furiously for a few seconds and then scribbled notes with a pen attached to a peacock feather.

Currant was taken aback, but took the hint. She went back to her desk and clicked the link to the **Mission, Vision, and Values** site that Stacey had emailed after Onboarding. Then she grabbed her mug and went for a refill. *Maybe I can catch her eye on the way back.*

She could not. Gianna remained steadfast in her focus, looking forcefully not at Currant.

Stop being stupid, Currant. If you need to talk to her, just talk to her. She stood up straight, walked directly to Gianna's desk, and smiled. "Hi, Gianna."

Gianna slowly looked up; she stared silently at Currant over the rims of her cat's eye glasses.

"Beck suggested that I sit down with you to get some insight into your role and to get to know you a little better. When would be a good time for us to chat?"

The prescription lenses magnified Gianna's eye-roll. Sighing, she clicked to her calendar. "First thing tomorrow morning."

"Okay, great! So, 9:00? 9:30?"

"I'll be in at 7:00," Gianna said. "I'm free till 8:00." She picked up her peacock pen and turned her back.

My first official work thing completed! Currant crossed it off the list and moved to her next To-Do.

During their discussion that morning, Beck had instructed her to review documents from a previous campaign's rollout before starting her in-store collateral project. "There's a whole folder somewhere," he had said. "On the S: Drive, maybe? I'm not sure. It was back in 2018 or 2019, so you'll have to dig."

Currant dug. A search for **rollout** produced no results, so she methodically scrolled through every document on the drive. She learned many interesting things—*So that's why the Appropriate Workplace Conversations e-learning* *module is mandatory. I wonder if HR knows you can password-protect files?* —but nothing related to her task. She made a note to ask Beck if he remembered any keywords that might help her track the folder down.

The afternoon wore on. Gianna packed up at 4:00, passing silently behind Currant's chair.

How long should I stay? I don't have anything to do.

Beck reappeared at 6:01, staring hard at his phone.

"Hey, Beck, quick question—"

He raised the phone to his ear and mouthed "Sorry—call." He grabbed the messenger bag from his desk and gave a quick salute. Currant watched out the window till Beck climbed into a Nissan Leaf, and then shut her computer down.

Chapter 12

On her third day at Alpine Chalet Coffee Company, Currant woke before the alarm clock and whistled through her morning routine. Business school had given her the tactical toolkit necessary to lead across power differentials, to build trust and buy-in, and if necessary, to thrive in suboptimal environments. The early-morning meeting with Gianna would be her first opportunity to implement.

Currant dressed quickly and was in the car by 6:15. Traffic was thin, so she arrived at the office at 6:45. She marched toward the building, heels rapping boldly through the stillness of the morning, and ran through her game plan. Gianna obviously felt threatened, which was understandable; Currant was young, well-educated, and already climbing the corporate ladder. She had likely been reacting from a place of insecurity when she treated Currant with condescension the day before.

Currant, then, would be respectful but firm and make it clear to Gianna that she would not be party to any power games. *I respect your experience and expertise, but I bring knowledge and a fresh perspective that can also be of value to the team*, she would say. *Let's find a way to work together.*

Currant's stride lengthened as she approached the main door, mentally focused and ready for battle. She reached the entryway and yanked the door handle firmly.

It was locked.

Shoot, she remembered. *It's badge access only from 7:00 PM to 7:00 AM.*

A pair of headlights turned into the parking lot. To avoid awkwardly tracking the driver from car to door, Currant dug through her bag, searching for a badge she knew wasn't there. As the footsteps approached, she looked up, ready to introduce herself as a new joiner and to tailgate inside.

"Good morning, baby girl! Let me get that door for you."

The badge reader beeped, and Gianna held the door open. They crossed the marble foyer, Gianna's heels clicking more loudly than Currant's. "Turn right!" Gianna instructed. "Caffeine first."

Currant followed her toward the Coffee Bar, the motion-activated office lights clicking on like spotlights as they walked down the hall.

"So how have your first two days been?" Gianna asked, with no hint of the previous afternoon's attitude.

"They've been good," Currant said guardedly. "Lots of information to absorb."

"I bet." Gianna set her giant designer bag on the Coffee Bar's counter. "What are you drinking?" she asked.

"I'll just have some coffee," Currant said automatically, and then realized that the commercial-grade, dual-burner, thirty-gallon-per-hour coffee machine had not yet been activated. *How do I use this thing?* She panicked. *I can't ask Gianna for help—that will shift the power differential even further in her favor.*

"Nope," said Gianna. "The first batch of the morning takes ten minutes to brew. You're having what I'm having—a Gianna Special." Currant complied, and a few minutes later, they headed back toward their wing, leaving row after row of buzzing fluorescent ceiling lights activated in their wake.

Currant had picked up speed as they approached the Marketini Lounge, determined to enter first so that she could claim the dominant position in the fuchsia armchair. *This is it*, she thought, putting her mug on the table and sitting straight and taut. *Go time.*

"Gianna?"

"Just turning on the lights, honey. Unless you *want* to have our meeting in the dark?"

"Oh." Currant looked around, noticing that the Marketini Lounge and the Visual Identity enclave were still in shadows. "I thought they were automatic."

"Our sensor's broken," Gianna said, stepping out of her stilettos. She reclined along the length of the sofa, bright red toenails pointing directly at Currant.

"So what should we talk about, honey?" Gianna reached leisurely for her coffee. "And what do you think of your Gianna Special?"

Currant took a sip. She was expecting something sickeningly sweet; double caramel hazelnut, maybe, or vanilla white chocolate raspberry. But she found the Gianna Special to be smooth and subtle—and very, very good. "What is this?" Currant asked, surprised.

"A girl's gotta have her secrets," Gianna said coyly.

Currant took another sip to gird her courage. She opened her mouth, ready to launch into her memorized lines.

Gianna interrupted her. "Let's do this. Why don't you tell me a little about yourself, I'll tell you a little about myself, and then we can talk about how we're going to work together. How does that sound?"

Currant closed her mouth, startled. But Gianna's proposal made sense, so she put her firm-but-fair speech on hold and gave an elongated elevator-pitch summary of her resume. "...and then my journey brought me here to Alpine Chalet, and to the Visual Identity team, where I'm really excited to leverage my education and experience to help communicate change and ultimately grow the business."

Then Gianna introduced herself. Still reclining, she took another sip of her coffee drink and told Currant that she'd been working in marketing for more than twenty years. "Probably about as long as you've been alive, baby girl." She had started her career at an architecture firm, worked for over a decade in advertising, and then joined Alpine Chalet Coffee Company just as it was making the transition from a few neighborhood coffee shops to a full-blown regional chain. Several promotions later, she was the Vice President of Marketing Special Projects.

"It's great to hear that you've been promoted several times," Currant said, showing Gianna that she was actively listening. "It sounds like AlChal has a strong focus on career-pathing and growth."

Gianna sat up, surprisingly gracefully, and narrowed her eyes. "I'd say that *I* have a strong focus on career-pathing and growth. One thing you need to learn, Currant—and the sooner, the better—is that your career is your own responsibility."

The abrupt change in behavior startled Currant. *Wow, I didn't mean to offend her.* "I didn't mean—"

Gianna cut her off.

"Nobody owes you anything in life, girl. You're on your own." Her words were pellets of ice, hard and sharp and chilling. "If you want to succeed, you have to be willing to do *whatever it takes.*"

Shivers coursed through Currant's shoulders at the intensity of Gianna's words. She wrapped her hands around her mug, desperate for its warmth.

Then the steel in Gianna's eyes gave way to the bright, bombastic status quo. "But, sure, honey, if you do a good job and make enough noise, you'll move up eventually! I was just a Marketing Coordinator when I started here, but look at me now." She gestured widely with a well-muscled arm. "I'm the Queen of Visual Identity!"

Currant smiled and asked Gianna to describe some of her proudest accomplishments. She made agreeable noises while Gianna chattered on about the campaigns she'd conceived and the branding work she'd done

I didn't just imagine that, did I? Currant thought, reflecting on the sea change in Gianna's mood that she had just witnessed. *That was legitimately weird.*

"So you created the red-and-white edelweiss badge Creative that's currently in use?" Currant heard herself ask.

"I sure did, honey," Gianna said, and raised one perfectly penciled eyebrow. "In fact, you could say that it's my greatest asset!" She laughed heartily, slapped her knees, and stood up. The meeting was over.

Currant's project was blocked until she spoke with Beck about the S: Drive documents, and he wasn't in yet. *I should learn about AlChal's operations so I'm fully up-to-speed once my project starts moving.* Currant spent the morning reading the intranet; there was lots of information to absorb.

Silence blanketed the Visual Identity enclave, punctuated periodically by clicking keys. She read through corporate statements on sustainability, fleet management, and customer-centered workflows in an almost meditative state, observing each policy and then letting it slide gently away. After a while, her eyelids drooped.

A cannon-blast of notification chimes exploded from her speakers, and Beck's voice boomed out from behind her. "Hey, Currant, did you get my invite?"

When her heart resumed beating, Currant checked her inbox. **Lunch Currant – Beck**, the calendar invitation read; **5 minutes**, said the reminder. She clicked 'Open' on the invite automatically: `Sorry we missed lunch on Monday – I was super sick – but let's do it today.`

"Sorry we missed lunch on Monday," Beck said. "I was super sick. But let's do it today."

Currant looked over to find him pushing back from his desk. He stood up and stretched, his untucked flannel rising up to expose a bit of belly. "Gianna, you in?"

Gianna took off her rhinestone-studded headphones and looked quizzically at Beck; he repeated the question, and she shook her head. Beck turned back to Currant. "Where should we go?"

Chapter 13

They ended up in Beck's Leaf, heading toward a clean-eating fast-casual restaurant a few miles away.

"How have your first two days been?" Beck asked over the soft electrical whir. His hands were at ten and two.

"They've been good," said Currant. "Lots of information to absorb."

Beck looked over at her quickly and flashed his big, white smile. "I bet." His eyes returned to the road.

I need to ask him about the S: Drive folder. "Hey, Beck, I meant to ask you about the documents from the previous rollout. I—"

"Nope, it's lunch time. No work talk! We're just hanging out, getting to know each other."

He came to a complete stop at an intersection and then ventured cautiously through. "What do you do for fun?"

Currant hated that question. *I sit on my couch and look at the internet* didn't completely align with the personal brand she was building, and she didn't have any well-defined hobbies. "I read quite a bit," she said. "And I'm interested in photography." She had bought a digital camera the previous year and had used it twice.

"Cool! I love photography. What do you shoot?"

I took that picture of the sunset once. "Mostly landscapes," she answered.

The restaurant was visible on the horizon, and she tried to steer the conversation back toward Beck before he asked for any more details. "What about you? What do *you* do for fun?"

"I don't have time for fun," Beck said, pulling carefully into a spot labeled **Electric Cars Only.** "Just kidding."

Currant laughed politely and they headed inside.

Their timing was perfect; there were only a few people ahead of them in line. They studied the menu board. "Have you been here before?" Currant asked.

"Nope, but Maria and Pamela from HR recommended it. I've heard it's awesome." So had half of the working population of the western suburbs, judging by the steady stream of people stacking up behind them. Suddenly, they were next, and the cashier was asking them impatiently for their order. Currant requested what she hoped would be a grilled chicken salad.

"And for you?" the cashier barked.

Beck froze. "Umm... the Handground Semolina Spaghettini with Cage-Free Carbonara, please." The cashier handed them a table number and they headed to an empty booth.

"You didn't get a chance to tell me what you do for fun," Currant prompted.

"Anything and everything," Beck answered, "As long as it's outdoors. If I'm not working, I'm usually in the woods. Hell, half the time I'm working, I'm in the woods. All you need these days is a hotspot and a VPN, you know?"

A harried server interrupted him. "Cage-Free Carbonara and a Super Greens Protein

Nurture Bowl?" He plopped the dishes down, transposed, and swept up their table number.

Currant handed over Beck's creamy, cheesy pile of pasta; she held tight to the smell of bacon as she accepted her bleak-looking salad. Beck said "Bon app," and they dug in, the silence only semi-awkward because they were eating.

Currant was eating, at least. Beck had only taken a couple of bites.

"Is your food okay?" Currant asked.

"Yeah, it's really good, but I'm trying to eat Keto." Beck sighed.

Then why did you order a giant bowl of spaghetti? Currant thought.

"I didn't want to ask for a bunch of substitutions, you know? I hate being that guy. But it's fine—I can just eat the sauce."

"What do you do in the woods?" Currant asked. *Ugh, that's a super weird question.* "I love the outdoors, too," she added quickly. "We have a family cabin up north on Lake Vermilion."

"Okay, sure. That's not too far from Sam Lake."

"Sam Lake?" Currant raised an eyebrow. "I've never heard of it."

"Really?" Beck seemed shocked. "You must not fish."

Currant shrugged. "So are you a big fisherman, then?"

"I've been known to wet a line," Beck said. "We were just up at Sam Lake Lodge for the annual C-Suite corporate fishing trip last weekend, and I brought home, like, a dozen walleyes." Currant was pretty sure the legal limit was six.

"I love walleye," she said. "My dad makes them with Shore Lunch and fried potatoes. Not exactly Keto-friendly, but incredibly good."

"*Yes*. I ordered that at this super backwoodsy place up north—Gavin recommended it—and it was such a vibe. Personally, I usually just do my walleye in a brown-butter sauté with a pinch of thyme, but I sous-vided a couple of fillets the other night and they turned out *amazing*."

"You must be quite the cook," Currant said, and Beck talked for several minutes about his Insta-Pot. Then Currant finished her remaining kale, and Beck twirled the last noodle around his fork. He pushed aside his empty dish and stood up.

"Well, we better get back. I have a one o'clock."

Chapter 14

Tension tightened Currant's shoulders as she woke her computer from hibernation the next morning. *Really? Nothing?*

Beck had been in back-to-back meetings after their lunch the previous afternoon, so Currant had emailed him to ask for guidance on her S: Drive search. He had not replied.

The empty hours yawned open in front of her. *What do I do now?*

In one ear came a cautious, careful whisper: *He specifically told me to start by reviewing these documents, and my first official act should not be disobedience. Plus, why reinvent the wheel? Those documents will save me a lot of time.*

In the other ear, fire and force: *I looked and didn't find anything; I asked for guidance and got*

x

no response. What am I supposed to do, just sit here and do nothing for the next week? And it's just ordering branded napkins, for God's sake—it's not rocket science.

But you don't know where to get the napkins! hissed the careful voice. *You can't just go to Vistaprint and order ten million napkins! And you don't even know how many napkins to order!*

Maybe not, but I can reason it out. It's just like the case interviews I prepared for when I wanted to go into consulting: How many ping pong balls would it take to fill a 747? How many gas stations are there in Kentucky? I just need to lay out my assumptions…

The battle raged internally as she went to fill her coffee mug.

When she got back, there were distractions in her inbox. Max and Karina were going on a burrito run; Jenna and Xander had already replied-all with their requests. The next email was a meeting invitation for 2:00 that afternoon. **Welcome with Gavin: Currant/**

Sung-Min/Purnima. Currant clicked 'Accept' on the invite, and then turned her attention to her burrito order.

Three hours and no progress later, she took the lone plastic salad container from among the foil-wrapped bundles and sat down next to Xander.

"What's that?" he asked.

"It's a carnitas bowl," Currant answered, reaching across the table for a beige disposable fork.

"That fork is biodegradable," Purnima said, with a mouth full of black beans. "It's made of corn."

"Huh," said Currant.

The group ate in silence for a few minutes. "What's everyone doing for Memorial weekend?" asked Jenna.

"Nothing much," answered Max. "Just chilling."

Currant swallowed a bite of pork. "We have a cabin up north, so I'm going to head up there."

"I'm going to explore Minneapolis," said Xander. "There seem to be some super cute little neighborhoods, especially up by the lakes. Really quaint."

They chatted for a few more minutes, and then Currant speared the last chunk of meat with her corn-fork.

Sung-Min pushed his chair back from the table. "Well," he said, "Back to work."

Currant watched the clock in the corner of her screen, bidding the minutes to pass faster. Surprisingly, they did; before she knew it, the meeting notification chimed. She grabbed her coffee mug and her notebook and hurried down the hall.

When she reached the leadership suite, Gavin's door was open. Currant had never seen a CEO's office before. She wasn't sure what she had been expecting—mahogany paneling and a life-sized oil portrait of the company's founder, maybe—but what she saw was a sparsely furnished space in shades of ivory, birch, and a warm, velvety taupe. The furniture was Scandinavian but clearly not Ikea, and a collection of coffee mugs, individually mounted, ringed the room like a model railroad.

Gavin himself seemed wholly absorbed in whatever was on his screen; Currant could see bar charts. *Should I wait, or should I just go in?* Purnima and Sung-Min were nowhere in sight. She checked her watch: 1:58. *I'm early, and he looks busy.* Currant slowly backed away.

"What are you doing?" Sung-Min had come up silently behind her.

"I'm—um—we're early."

Purnima rounded the corner. "What's going on?" she said. Sung-Min shrugged.

Gavin looked up to see them huddled in his doorframe. "Hey," he said softly, locking his computer and pushing his chair back. "Please—come in."

Like any good job candidate, Currant had done her research on Alpine Chalet Coffee Company's leadership team. She had read Gavin's bio on the website, and had even skimmed a couple of profile pieces in a local business magazine. She knew that he was originally from northern Minnesota, had gotten his start at McKinsey, and had helped multiple mid-sized QSR chains to scale. She was not, however, prepared for the reality of the man emerging from behind the broad birch desk.

His presence was electric. He said nothing, just smiled, and his energy enveloped the three LATTE participants. Currant felt safe and warm, almost amniotic, as she sank into the Danish modern side chair.

"Hi," said Gavin Woodrow, and then, "Wow." One long look at the gathered group, a beat of eye contact with each of them, and a serene, unhurried smile. "So this is the future of Alpine Chalet Coffee Company." A few more beats of silence, and again, "Wow."

Currant felt herself leaning toward him and noticed her colleagues were doing the same.

"Stacey told me I was going to be impressed, but I had no idea." He paused. "Purnima, what an incredible CV. Stanford is a great school—I went there, too."

Purnima sat up even straighter.

"Sung-Min, with your crypto portfolio, you don't need to work at all. We were lucky to get you."

Sung-Min grinned bashfully.

"And Currant…" Gavin's eyes locked on hers and the room faded away. "You have the most directly applicable experience in the whole group. I've never worked frontline in the quick-service-restaurant industry like you have, but I *did* start out behind the counter at the Savings & Loan my father headed. I know that working face-to-face with customers can give you an understanding into the human psyche that even the best business school can't match."

Gavin leaned back slightly to address all three new MBAs. "I'm so glad you're here."

That was a collective 'you', Currant noted rationally, but her heart trilled all the same.

"… and I know you share this vision for AlChal's future. Let me just say quickly, before we finish, that I'm so glad you're on this journey—that we're on this journey *together*—and I can't wait to see how far we'll go." Gavin smiled his languid, light-filled smile and rose from his office chair.

Currant looked around, startled; the clock on the wall said twenty minutes had gone by. Sung-Min and Purnima were pushing back and standing up; the meeting was coming to an end. Currant gathered her notebook and coffee mug, slowly, while gazing around the room.

Gavin stood by the door and shook hands with each of them as they filed past. His smile was radiant, his grip firm but tender, and Currant wanted to stay in that moment forever.

Her eyes lit upon one of the coffee mugs mounted on the wall; it was blaze orange, emblazoned with a walleye, and said **Sam Lake Lodge** on the side. "Do you fish?" Currant asked Gavin, trying to prolong the moment.

"No, I don't," he said, eyes boring into hers. He paused for just a millisecond. "I hunt."

Then his luminous smile returned, and he gave a slight bow and a wave. "Thank you all, again, for being here," he said to the group. "Know that I appreciate each one of you."

The three LATTE participants, basking in his glow, walked in serene, balmy silence to their desks.

When his door clicked shut, Gavin's smile snapped off; it had served its purpose and was no longer necessary. His tranquil, golden warmth turned to icy intensity as he turned his attention toward his next task.

Chapter 15

At 7:02 the next morning, Currant opened up *FullDayDinInstoreCollatTracker.xlsx*.

She had started the spreadsheet, and finished half of its tasks, during a slightly manic period of productivity the afternoon before.

After leaving Gavin's presence, she had gone back to her desk and *worked*. S: Drive documents be damned—nothing could have held her back. It was nearly 7:00 PM when she clicked **Save** and then **Shut Down**, and she continued thinking about her rollout until she fell asleep.

Now, with fresh eyes and new ideas, she picked up where she had left off. Her spreadsheet glittered with conditional formatting, highlighting optimums based on minimum order quantities, batch-dependent price breaks, and preferred vendor scores. She tested one last formula, watched the desired cell light up in a reassuring pine-tree green, and grinned. *Done!* And it was only 8:15.

True, she had recoiled a bit when Beck first described the project, because it sounded lowly and boring and small. But after an attitude reboot the previous afternoon—*don't look down, look above and beyond!*—she had enhanced the project scope. The tactical execution posed little intellectual challenge, and she was confident that her spreadsheet had addressed that. What really excited Currant now were the strategic possibilities.

She had a page full of nightstand scribbles from the previous evening: ideas for a complementary merchandising concept and an internal rollout plan. She could feel the potential in these workstreams and couldn't wait to turn them kinetic. All she needed was Beck's buy-in.

Currant closed Excel and opened up PowerPoint.

Beck came in around 10:00 AM. He stalked straight to his desk and plopped his messenger bag down loudly.

"Good morning," Currant said. "When you have a few minutes, I'd love to run something by you."

Beck held up his hand. "I had a rough night, and I'm not a morning person on the best of days. Can we talk in half an hour? The coffee should have kicked in by then."

"Sure, sounds perfect," she said, cheerfully but not too loud.

It was forty-five minutes before Beck was ready. He pinged her, the intra-office messenger window flashing in the corner of the screen.

is now good?

Currant turned around to look at Beck, who was sitting seven feet away from her. He had headphones on, similar to Gianna's, but un-Bedazzled.

Sure, replied Currant.

cool, let's go to the marketini lounge

Beck took the fuchsia armchair. "Okay, what do you have for me?"

Currant's presentation was already in full-screen mode, and she twirled her laptop to face Beck.

"Just really quick, before we begin," Beck said, "I have a hard stop at 11:00."

Currant said that she would be brief and hoped he could hear her over the pounding of her heart. This was her first official presentation for her first official task at her first official job. The excitement she'd felt earlier melted like candlewax. *What if it's terrible? What if he looks at this and thinks I'm a stupid little kid who knows nothing about business? What if I am a stupid little kid who knows nothing about business?* Before she could chicken out, she clicked the Forward arrow and got started.

Currant thought back to the Presentation Skills workshop that she'd done during her MBA: 'Tell them what you're going to say, say it, then summarize what you've said'.

"I'm going to walk you through what I've put together in terms of generating awareness for our Full-Day Dining Initiative," Currant began. "First, I'd like to go through an expanded merchandising concept, then I'd like to discuss the actual rollout approach, and at the end, I've got an idea for a potential addition to the campaign that I'd love to float past you."

Tell him what you're going to say: Check.

She flipped to the next slide. Her header read **Expand branded merchandising SKUs outside of traditional "Morning" items**.

"First of all, the merchandising concept. From what I understand, traditionally, the majority of the branded merchandise in the Chalet Shop has been drinkware—coffee mugs, travelers, etc. But since the whole point of the Full-Day Dining Initiative is to break out of the morning-only mold, I think we need to complement our current offering with new product lines."

Beck's phone vibrated loudly on the coffee table. Currant barely registered it.

"We'll still do some mugware, of course, but I think we should fully embrace the Office-Away-From-Office concept. I'm thinking USB drives, Moleskine-type notebooks, reusable water bottles... all the things that clutter up your desk at work. Our goal should be to get our guests to associate AlChal with their workday."

Currant finally took a breath. She realized she had been staring at the screen as she'd been speaking, and now looked to Beck to gauge his reaction. His head was down, staring at his phone.

He realized she was looking at him, looked up—still typing with his thumbs—and said, "Right. Non-food revenue is a relatively small component of the top line, but since the margin is so high, it has a disproportionate impact on EBITDA. Maximizing our return here is going to be key to the overall success of the launch."

Currant wasn't sure what to do with that information. She hesitated, thinking, but Beck didn't seem to expect a response. She pressed on.

"Next up is the rollout approach. Now, the external rollout is arguably the most important, since encouraging engagement and additional spend from our customers is really what this is all about. However, I think we'd be remiss to exclude one of our most valuable stakeholder groups: employees. I propose we do an *internal* rollout to build engagement here at AlChal first, and then use that momentum to carry us forward into a successful external launch."

Beck was paying closer attention now.

"First of all, the major change that we're introducing here is the expanded menu—so we need to get our employees on board. Let's schedule the rollout for noon; we'll bring in a tasting menu of our new dishes and cater lunch for the whole office."

"Great thought," Beck said. "It's always important to stand behind your product, and we historically haven't done enough dogfooding. Getting a taste of our own products is an awesome idea."

Currant nodded. "Now, to bring in the merchandising concept and to cement the outdoorsy vibe, we'll take a cue from Gianna's new Creative and serve lunch off of enamelware. I've found a party rental company that can furnish the place settings." She clicked forward to a photo of a red-speckled plate and mug flanked by a stainless-steel spork and butter knife.

"Then I thought we'd expedite the first set of enamelware mugs with the new brand asset so we could give one to each employee during the internal rollout. That way we can keep the initiative top-of-mind even after the launch event is over."

So far, so good, Currant thought. She was halfway through her first real-life business presentation, and she hadn't been laughed at by her boss a single time. Fortified, she clicked onward.

"I love the new logo, and obviously that will be the *visual* centerpiece of both rollouts. But I say we take that even a step further and engage the other senses, as well." *This is it…* Currant thought. *The coup de grace.*

Beck's phone vibrated again, but he ignored it.

"For the internal rollout, what if we have an actual campfire? We could set it up in the parking lot. We'd get the sound of the crackling fire, the feel of the heat on your skin, and the smell of the wood smoke. We could even—"

"We could make S'mores!" Beck said, practically shouting. "And roast hot dogs!"

Currant was a bit taken aback by his enthusiasm but decided to roll with it.

"Absolutely. I mean, we still want the focus of the rollout lunch to be our new Full-Day Dining menu so our colleagues get a sense of the dishes that we'll be offering to our customers, but supplementing that with—"

"What about Foil Packet Bananas? You know, where you wrap up bananas and chocolate and cook them over the campfire? We'll already have the chocolate for the S'mores."

Bemused, Currant nodded. "We… could do that."

She clicked to the next slide before he could continue. "I want to be mindful of your time, so let's quickly run through the external rollout plan. Similar to the concept of engaging the senses at the internal rollout, we want to market to customers from multiple angles. The imagery in the new Creative will trigger the visual centers of the brain, but we want to trigger the linguistic centers, as well. A tagline that ties to the imagery will cement the brand identity even further. Here's my proposal."

She clicked again and the campfire design filled the screen; another click, and **Fuel Your**

Fire appeared beneath it. She paused for a moment to let it sink in.

"Our customers have passions, things that drive them—but they need resources to fuel those passions. AlChal provides those resources, whether literally—caffeine and calories—or figuratively—a warm, inviting, office-like environment. To me, this tagline conveys exactly what we are trying to achieve with the Full-Day Dining Initiative."

Currant clicked out of the presentation and looked timidly at Beck. "So, those were my thoughts."

"Love it," Beck said. "Love it, love it, love it. *Fuel Your Fire*? Bam. That's it, right there." His wide, whiskered grin sharpened his chiseled jawline even further.

Currant couldn't help herself; she grinned back. *Nailed it!*

"Now," Beck said, back to business. "We probably need a vegan alternative. What do you think about Quorn Dogs? Would those work over a campfire? Are they firm enough to be skewered?"

Chapter 16

The next morning, Currant was in the car before the sun came up. It was a five-hour drive from Saint Paul to the cabin, and she looked forward to it every time. Suburbs gave way to farmland, then forests, as she drove northward; the same old landmarks, timeless and familiar, ticked off the distance just as surely as the mile markers. She passed Hinckley, halfway between the Twin Cities and cabin country, known for its casino and its caramel rolls. She stopped for gas where she always stopped for gas, at a filling station in Barnum in the shadow of Big Louie, a 25-foot fiberglass voyageur. She saw the hand-lettered political rants outside of Cotton, unchanging sentiments painted fresh each spring, and checked off the little cities that she left in her rear view: Virginia, Eveleth, Mountain Iron.

Her mind wandered back through her first week at work.

I've faced adversity, obstacles, and difficult personalities, just like business school warned me I would. She reflected on her truncated first day, on the tension with Gianna, and on her project. Then she brightened, remembering her presentation to Beck. *Nevertheless, I persisted,* she thought, *and I'm already making an impact.*

Currant turned off the highway onto the gravel road that would lead her toward the lake.

Her great-grandfather had built the family's cabin more than eighty years earlier. He had settled in northern Minnesota because the flora and fauna reminded him of his native Liechtenstein. There, he'd been a humble carpenter, but America was the land of promise; after immigrating, he built up a successful lumber business and did very well for himself.

So well, in fact, that he bought a small island on Lake Vermilion, the most scenic of Minnesota's ten-thousand-plus lakes. He cleared the island's western half and used the timber to frame up a modest cabin with a grandiose view. He also built a boathouse on the water, almost as big as the cabin itself, facing the mainland.

One glorious Saturday morning in spring 1927, he motored his wife and their two sons a few hundred yards across Silent Man Bay and docked a gleaming new Chris-Craft in the boathouse. There had been Kepplers on Keppler Island almost every weekend since. This weekend, the unofficial opening of the summer cabin season, the entire family would be congregating; there would be swimming and boat rides and good food and drink, and Currant couldn't wait.

The rumble of the road abated as she turned into the lot of Silent Man Landing Bait Shop & Convenience. She parked between her cousin

Matt's dark blue Durango and her father's F-150, unfolded herself from the front seat, and grabbed her duffel bag.

The string of bells above the door tinkled. "Hi, Currant! Happy Memorial Day weekend!" said the white-haired man behind the counter.

"Hi, Mr. Hakkala! Same to you. How's the season looking? Busy yet?" She had long been instructed to use his first name, but he had been 'Mr. Hakkala' to Currant since she was old enough to talk, and his name wasn't going to change now.

"Can't complain. The ice was out early this year, and we had quite a few people through for fishing opener two weekends ago."

They chatted for a few more minutes; he congratulated her on her MBA and Currant told him about her job at Alpine Chalet Coffee Company.

"… so I probably won't be able to make it up here as often this summer," she said.

"Just remember, Currant, there's more to life than work."

"Yeah, Mr. Hakkala?" She looked around the shop, a bustling little operation that he had built up since retiring in his mid-forties from a successful career in criminal defense. The bait shop, he'd told her once, was a hobby, something to keep him busy.

Mr. Hakkala laughed, a big Santa laugh that Currant had always loved. "This isn't work," he said. "My whole life is a vacation."

"Well, no one's left a boat for you," he continued. "Do you want to call over and see if someone will come get you?" He handed her the phone, its long, curly cord extending over the scarred linoleum counter.

In the early days of mobile phones, reception in this part of the state had been spotty. Now, Currant had full bars, but she would no more have used her cell than she would have called Mr. Hakkala 'Arnie'.

"Hi, Aunt Kay! Yep. Sure. Do we need anything from the store? Okay. Chunky or creamy? Okay. Yeah, sure. Yep. Bye!" She passed the phone back across the counter.

Ice, peanut butter, minnows, mail. Ice, peanut butter, minnows, mail. Currant beelined to the middle shelf of the third aisle. She grabbed a jar, thought better of it and grabbed two, and then headed toward the bait tanks. By the time she got back up to the counter, they could hear the whine of a boat motor.

Currant tucked the peanut butter into her purse and stepped out into the sun. She crossed the parking lot to a bank of mailboxes that served cabins all up and down the point. From the one labeled "Keppler", she pulled out a National Geographic and an issue of the Cretin County Gazette. She scanned the local headlines as she made her way back toward the water.

Aunt Kay had pulled a beat-up old rowboat with a much-newer outboard alongside the dock. "Hey, Currant!" She accepted the minnows and ice that Currant handed over.

"Hi, Aunt Kay!" Currant threw her duffel into the bottom of the boat and climbed aboard. "How's it going?"

Aunt Kay backed away from the dock as Currant settled onto the splintered wooden bench. She might have answered, but her words were lost in the chop as she opened up the motor and sped them across Silent Man Bay. Dock to dock was only a couple of hundred yards, and soon Currant pushed through the screen door of the cabin, letting it slam behind her.

"Currant!" said her Uncle Mitchell, wiping his hands on a dish towel, and her mother came down the stairs from the second floor. Her cousin Matt put down the novel he'd been reading, and her grandfather put down his Old Fashioned. There were hugs all around.

Up here, she wasn't Currant Keppler, LATTE Management Rotation Program participant at Alpine Chalet Coffee Company; she was just Currant, eight or twelve or twenty-four, surrounded by pine trees and lake water and the people who loved her most in the world. Nestled on the island that felt more like home than home did, Currant finally felt herself relax.

Chapter 17

Early morning, Memorial Day, Currant walked down to the lake with her final cabin coffee. The sun was up, and the woods were waking; it was peaceful, but not quiet. A loon was singing an early morning aria; a chickadee and a squirrel chattered over each other in tumbling harmony. The waves lapped steadily at the shore in rhythm, and the hum of a boat motor in the distance underscored it all like the drone on a bagpipe.

Currant sat back on a bench that her grandmother had built and closed her eyes to listen. The lake, the island, the animals— they had all been here long before the Keppler camp, and the camp had been here a long time already.

She had grown older, and her world had grown more complicated, but the island never changed. It was a silver thread, spanning past, present, and future, and there was comfort in its constancy. Currant breathed deep and took it all in and felt, for a moment, timeless.

Then she snapped her eyes open and looked at her watch. It was time to leave.

Her grandfather brought her back to her car in the pontoon. At the landing, she jumped out with her duffel.

"Bye, Grandpa!" she called as he motored away. She could see her mother, just visible at the end of the dock on the other side of Silent Man Bay, waving. Currant waved back, and then crunched across the gravel toward her Honda.

She got in the car, took her phone from her purse, and plugged it in to the car charger. She had a new text from Luke, asking if she'd like to meet him that evening at a swanky downtown bar.

I'll be there, she replied.

The calm and connection that she had felt on Keppler Island held on only for a few miles. She was heading south, back toward the Cities and Luke Kennedy and Alpine Chalet Coffee Company. Currant drove on autopilot, eyes fixed on the horizon.

Her landmarks ticked by, vying for her attention, but were they leading her closer to the future or tethering her to the past? Currant flashed on a motivational tweet she'd seen recently: **Value tradition, but favor growth**. Currant wanted to grow.

Growth meant change, and change was good. Disruption was necessary to top the market; agility and constant innovation were imperative to success. *New*, she thought. *Creative. At work and in life, that should be my mantra.*

Currant pulled onto the shoulder and reached for her phone, ready to open up the Maps app. She hesitated, then opened the glove compartment instead. She unfolded a road map of the state of Minnesota, pinpointed her location, and plotted a different route home. Ten minutes later, after taking a turn-off that she had passed a hundred times previously, Currant was on a road that she had never been down before.

The landscape looked similar to her normal route, but unlike the interstate, the county highway was buttressed by houses and homesteads and the occasional body shop. She drove past towns that she had heard of and a couple she hadn't, and almost turned down a little road that promised a Toy Soldier and Model Railroad Museum—*Exact Replica of 1937 DM&IR Line!* Instead, she filed it away for future reference and maintained her bearing toward home.

An hour in, Currant swallowed the last of her travel-mug coffee and recognized one flaw in her plan: there were no pre-defined pitstops on an unblazed trail. But just ahead was a small town and a small-town diner: Poppel Township, according to the Welcome sign, and the Camp Out Café, according to the faded letters spaced along the building's roof line.

The paint was flaking off the wooden siding and the parking lot was pocked and potholed, but a red-neon Open sign shone warmly from the window. She put on her blinker, slowed, and pulled off the highway.

She was expecting the tinkle of a welcome bell like at the Bait Shop, so the grating digital chirp of the door sensor irritated her. Currant nodded hello to two old men sitting on stools at the counter, and then slid into the farthest of the four booths, all of them optimistically set with paper placemats, mugs, and silverware.

A large, ruddy man peered out from the pass-through window, then pushed out of the swinging plastic kitchen doors. He wiped his hands on a stained apron, grabbed a menu off a stack and a coffee pot off a burner, and lumbered over to where Currant sat.

"Hi, there." His polo shirt said *Paul* where it peeked out from his apron and a whiff of whiskey clung to his breath. He held up the coffee pot and nodded down at the table.

Currant flipped her mug over onto its saucer, noticing a chip on its rim.

He poured the coffee, then asked, "You eating, too?"

"Yeah, I'll take a look," she said, accepting the laminated menu card.

"Okay. I'll be back in a minute, then." Paul returned to the counter and topped up the two men's mugs.

Pancakes. Pancakes sounded really good, and she was still technically on vacation, so calories were not a consideration yet. "I'll do the Short Stack," Currant called over to him, to save him a trip.

"Sure thing," Paul said and trundled back toward the kitchen.

Currant had left her phone charging in the car, so she read through the placemat. It was quintessentially small-town, sponsored by the local newspaper and full of advertisements for local businesses, fill-in-the-letter puzzles, high school sports schedules, and the occasional Bible verse.

She successfully solved the Fish Finder Puzzle, sponsored by Northern Lights Sports in Swan River, ('W_LL_YE'; 'M_SK__'; '_UN_ IS_'; 'CR_P_ _E') and noted duly that Thousand Lakes Savings & Loan was her preferred partner for personal, boat, and business loans throughout northeastern Minnesota.

"Headed home after the long weekend?"

The two men at the counter had swiveled on their stools to face her. They were dressed identically in faded jeans and short-sleeved work shirts. One had a yellow feed cap, and the other wore green.

"Yep," Currant said. "Gotta work tomorrow." *And I have a date.*

"You got a cabin up here then?" the yellow-hatted man asked.

"We have a place up on Vermilion," Currant answered. "I always take the interstate, so I thought I'd change things up a bit and take a different route home."

The more weathered of the two men nodded. "Good thing, too," Green Hat said. "This place woulda shut down a long time ago without Cities people like yourself."

"Aw, I'm doing okay." Paul had reemerged from the kitchen. He plopped a plate of pancakes down in front of Currant. "I'll be even better once I get the remodel going."

"You're remodeling?" Currant asked, more out of a duty to keep the conversation going than anything. *Not a bad idea*, she thought, surveying the outdated interior. The restaurant had all of the trappings of a vintage 1950s diner, but it was worn and chipped and dingy. What should have been classic just looked tired.

Paul's face, similarly tired, lit up; it was the first time he'd smiled since she entered the diner. "Yeah," Paul said. "Top to bottom."

"Uh oh," said Yellow Hat. "Now you've done it."

Paul reached across and fished under the counter, pulling out a thick, glossy green folder embossed with the Thousand Lakes Savings & Loan logo. He slid into the booth opposite Currant and took out an artist's sketch of a bright new interior.

The color scheme would be crimson and fawn, with accents of a deep, steely blue; it evoked the classic red vinyl and chrome aesthetic of a roadside diner, but carried a cooler, modern undertone. It perfectly captured the vintage aura that lay underneath the Café's grime.

"That looks great," Currant mumbled, mouth full of pancakes. "…and these pancakes are great."

"Manter makes the best pancakes in the state," Yellow Hat called from the counter.

"If only more people knew about them…" He elbowed Green Hat, who hid a smile.

"Exactly. I have *got* to start driving more traffic in here." Paul took the bait and pulled another sheaf from the Savings & Loan folder, which Currant recognized as a business plan.

"I put together some marketing ideas…" Paul said, flipping through a couple of pages. "See?"

He rotated the business plan toward Currant, and she could see a bullet-pointed list. 'Advertisement in Cretin County Gazette (including hospitality placemats)' read the first item. The list also included a new turn-off sign at a nearby highway junction, a website, and a sponsorship panel on the local high school's hockey rink.

"I'm rebranding, too."

"Oh, yeah? I'm actually in Visual Identity myself," Currant said, taking another bite of pancake.

Then she nearly choked.

Paul had flipped another page. On it, in all its wispy, bold vitality, was the Alpine Chalet Coffee Company Full-Day Dining Initiative logo.

Chapter 18

He stole our logo!

The design staring up at her was identical to the Creative that Currant was in charge of rolling out for the Lunch Launch. The colors were slightly different, softer and cooler, but the elements were all there: the campfire, the enamelware mug, even the steamy, wispy letters.

Currant managed to swallow her mouthful of pancake, but couldn't suppress her alarm. *How did he get this?*

She had been careful not to print the logo out, and had only uploaded vector files to a handful of legit-looking vendors. Had one of them leaked the design? Had Paul Manter paid for it? Or had he somehow breached Alpine

Chalet Coffee Company's secure internal network to access the file? *Am I eating the pancakes of a mastermind of corporate espionage?*

"What do you think?"

Currant forced herself to look Paul in the eye. "It's... incredible."

He beamed. "Thanks. I'm really proud of it."

"So, um, where did you find it?"

"I drew it," Paul said.

Currant's mouth fell open. *Wait... so we stole it from him?*

Paul interpreted her shock as awe, and his chest puffed with pride. "I was an art major at the U."

A snort came from the counter.

"Well, Sig, we can't all be fourth-generation bachelor farmers," Paul retorted. "Plus—see? It's paying off."

He turned another page in the business plan. "I'm going to order a big new neon sign, and then all new uniforms, coffee mugs, the whole works. Just have to wait for the loan to come through."

Currant smiled weakly. "Don't forget pens," she said. "People walk away with pens all the time, and it's one of the cheapest costs-per-impression you can get."

Currant dialed her mom as soon as she got back in her car. In place of a ring tone, she got silence; no service. She pulled away from the Camp Out Café and tried to work through the problem on her own.

Fact: The Camp Out Café's logo was almost identical to the Full-Day Dining Initiative logo. The similarities could not be coincidence.

Fact: Currant had been careful not to leak the design, and Paul had seemed sincere when he told her he had drawn it.

Conclusion: My brand-new MBA job is plastering stolen intellectual property on tumblers. Currant's face crumpled.

What do I do now? Should I report it? What happens if I do? Will I get in trouble? Maybe I'll get fired. Maybe we'll get sued. Am I an accessory?

The county highway curved suddenly, and she stomped the brakes. Her mind was going a mile a minute, and her Honda had been following suit.

Currant slowed herself down. *Analyze the situation.* Her Corporate Ethics class had been taught by a moral philosophy professor, so they had never touched on anything more concrete than the trolley problem, but she tried to think rationally.

AlChal is not an evil company. They bought coffee beans from all sorts of developing countries and were committed to following strict fair-trade and sustainability practices. They supported hundreds of small family farms throughout the southern hemisphere, even building schools in the communities where their growers lived. Plus, they donated a percentage of their profits to good causes. As ethical violations go, this one was minor.

If there was one thing she had learned during her MBA, it's that there was nothing new under the sun. Hundreds of frameworks for the same basic concepts, thousands of books for the same common sense. "All art is imitation", as the saying went, and "imitation is the sincerest form of flattery". Paul should be pleased that his design was worthy of a multi-region rollout.

She talked herself down as the miles ticked by. *I'm overreacting*, she thought. *This is probably normal. I'm in the big leagues now; I guess this is just how the game is played.*

As she approached the outer-ring suburbs, Currant pushed aside her concern over the logo; she had more important things to worry about. Tonight's meeting with Luke was Date Number Three, and she didn't know what the evening might bring. *Expect nothing, but plan for everything*, she thought. When she got home, she placed a candle by her bed and a travel toothbrush in her purse.

Chapter 19

Luke sat at the bar behind two squat copper mugs. There was an empty bar stool next to him, and Currant slid onto it. "Hey," she said.

"Hey!" He swiveled to face her, and the momentum of the spin brought his knees knocking into hers. He steadied himself with a hand on Currant's thigh and grinned. "They have a Memorial Monday special: Two-for-ones on anything that starts with M."

"That's creative," Currant said.

"Yeah. I mean, it's ironic, of course." Luke pointed to a laminated card with the words **Back-to-Back World War Champs!** in military stencil print. "You drink beer, right? They have Modelo, Molson Canadian, Murphy's Irish Stout…"

The bartender approached and cocked an eyebrow at Currant.

"Manhattans, please, with Maker's."

"…and a couple more Moscows for me," said Luke. Then *he* cocked an eyebrow at Currant. "Whoa. Whiskey. I like that."

Currant blushed.

"How was your weekend?" Luke asked.

Great, except for finding out that I work for IP thieves. "Great, except…"

She hesitated. The last thing she wanted was for Luke to think she was a naive little girl who couldn't handle business.

"Except…?" prompted Luke.

"Except I got a sunburn in a place that doesn't normally see the sun." *Ugh, Currant, why did you say that? It's dumb AND it's disprovable.*

"Hmmm," said Luke, grinning again. "That's no good. Maybe you need some aloe."

Currant grimaced at the line, but she hadn't given him much to work with. Luckily, the drinks arrived. They cheered, Luke's copper mug knocking against Currant's lowball with a dampened clunk.

"How was *your* weekend?" Currant asked, after a very large sip.

"Great," said Luke. "No 'except'. I spent the entire weekend on Zoom with my developer in Russia—that's why I'm drinking vodka tonight—but we finally have a working prototype of Regulr!"

"That's amazing!" said Currant.

Luke pulled out his phone. "It really is. You have no idea how hard it is to get something like this off the ground, Currant. I literally worked, like, sixty hours a week last week to shepherd this over the finish line."

"I worked sixty hours last week, too," Currant said. *Don't sound so indignant. It's not a competition.*

Luke didn't notice. He swiveled again on his barstool, and Currant swiveled, too. They faced each other, knees intertwined.

"See?" He held out his phone.

```
Hello, Luke Kennedy. Welcome
to $ESTAB_NAME! What'll it
be tonight - GIN & TONIC,
GINTONIC1, something else, or
see specials?
```

"Wow." Currant said, focused on the fact that his leg was between her legs.

"See how it says 'tonight'? It's looking at the system time on my device. It can also say 'this afternoon' and 'this morning'."

"That's cool."

"Yeah, and if I tap 'see specials', it will tell me what the specials are, and if I tap 'something else', it will take me to a menu. I can also tap here on 'Custom'..."

Luke tapped, and a screen full of icons popped up. "Here, you can create your own signature drink. If I tap on the Moonshine Jug, it gives me a dropdown of base alcohols. If I tap on the Cola Bottle, it lets me select a mixer, and if I tap on the Lemon Slice, I can choose my garnishes."

"The UI looks great," said Currant. "But you could think about matching the fonts and the accent colors with the rest of the app to make your brand even stronger."

"Yeah, I had a different freelancer build this module in parallel so I didn't lose time, but it's a good point. I'll have Stanislav stitch it together when he's cleaning up the front end."

Luke showed her a couple more features, each one with its own look and feel. Currant finished her first Manhattan and reached for her second.

"I'm also working on push notifications— you'll get an alert when it's Last Call for Happy Hour, for instance—but that's turning out to be non-trivial. It's one thing for a bar to input their closing time, since that doesn't vary, but Happy Hours seem to be a bit more fluid. It's super hard to automate."

"I bet," murmured Currant.

"Nevertheless, I'm persevering," Luke said. "But enough about me. How are *you*, Currant? How's corporate life?"

Before she could answer, the bartender bustled over. "Last call for Happy Hour. You two want to put in an order?"

Currant sighed. "I better not—I drove."

"Where'd you park?" Luke asked.

"In the garage across the street."

"You can park there overnight for $6, as long as you're out by 8:00 AM." Luke's hand found her thigh under the bar, and he trailed his fingers upward. "We'll have you back by 7:30."

He ordered them both another round.

I'm going home with Luke Kennedy.

Her face flushed as the realization washed over her. She reached for her glass, gulping down the whiskey-flavored water and melted ice in a bid to combat the heat in her cheeks.

She tried to act casual. "Corporate life's been good so far," she told him. "There've been some challenges, but overall, I can't complain."

"There are always challenges, even in entrepreneurship," Luke said. "*Especially* in entrepreneurship."

"Yeah?" Currant said. "What challenges have you been facing?"

"Concentration, for one thing. I've been thinking about you a lot, Currant."

Currant's face flushed even more.

Luke's eyes locked on hers, and he leaned slightly forward.

Currant leaned slightly forward.

The bartender leaned slightly forward, reaching over the bar top to place their drinks squarely in between them. "Couple more Moscows and Manhattans," he said. "Cheers."

"Thanks," Luke said, picking up a copper mug. He turned back toward Currant. "Actually, though, my biggest challenge is funding."

"Did you ever enter our Pitch Contest?" Currant asked.

"I did, now that you mention it," Luke said. "You didn't see my entry?" He took a sip of his drink.

"No, Xander's in charge of the applicant and judge workstream. I'm doing the marketing strategy."

"That's cool—you'll be good at that. I mean, you'd be good at anything…" He flashed his bright white grin at Currant. "Do you need any tips?"

They chatted for a few minutes about micro-branding and nano-influencers, and then Luke put a finger to her lips. "Enough about business." He leaned toward Currant, she leaned toward him, and this time, there were no interruptions.

Three-point-five Manhattans had lowered Currant's inhibitions, but the kiss was intense and they were in public. After several long, languid seconds, she pulled herself away.

Luke smiled at her, and she smiled back. "Your lipstick is smeared," he said.

Currant washed her hands in the hammered copper sink and then reapplied her lipstick. Bar bathrooms always had the best lighting, and with her glossy lips and sparkling eyes, she felt almost worthy of the company she was returning to.

Luke was framed in her sightline as she crossed back to the bar, the shadows sharpening his chiseled jawline. *He should be sculpted,* Currant thought. With his head bent low, looking down at his phone, he was a sexy, modern-day *Thinker.*

As she slid back onto the barstool, Luke locked his phone and looked up at her. His easy smile was gone; worry lines furrowed on his brow.

"What's wrong?" Currant asked.

"Stanislav just pinged me and said that there's an issue with the JSON. It's not carrying emojis correctly, and that's a key element in our user engagement."

"Oh, no," said Currant.

"That workstream has a *ton* of dependencies, and Stan's not what you'd call a big-picture guy. He's going to need my guidance."

Luke pulled out his wallet and signaled to the bartender. "I am *so* sorry to do this, Currant… I was really looking forward to this evening." He trailed his finger from her elbow to her index finger, and then took her hand. "But you get it, right? You get *me*."

"Of course," said Currant, a shade too brightly. "I completely get it."

The bartender came over with the tab, and Luke scribbled a quick signature.

"Great. My Uber just pulled up. I'll call you!"

She had half a drink left, but no reason to stay. Two large sips later, Currant slipped off her barstool, only slightly unsteadily, and headed for the door.

The evening sun off the tinted glass skyscrapers cast the downtown streets in gold. She walked past the parking garage with a pang of regret and made her way to the Light Rail station. She stepped on the train, then watched out the window as Minneapolis faded into Saint Paul.

Back at her apartment, Currant got ready for bed. The candle on the nightstand seemed disappointed not to be needed, and she was feeling frivolous, so she lit it before brushing her teeth. She read by candlelight for a little while and then replayed the evening's events. *I've been thinking about you a lot*, Luke had said, and *You get me*. She smiled to herself, watching the candle's flame dance, and then blew it out and went to sleep.

Chapter 20

Two hundred miles north, Paul Manter was sleeping, too.

The darkness was deep in Poppel Township. Night creatures were out—raccoons, fox, someone's old barn cat—moving silently amidst the tall grass and wildflowers at the side of the highway. The Field Forget-Me-Nots, usually a joyful pop of indigo against the emerald green, were a somber, muted blue. The crisp Minnesota air smelled of pine forest and wood smoke, cut by the cloying scent of gasoline.

The night was cool, but Paul was warm. He dreamed, scenes from his childhood, frigid winter nights near the woodburning stove. The amber twinkling from behind tempered glass mesmerized him, soothed him, lulled him to sleep.

No, stay awake. He had something to do, something to fix, something left undone. But his memories beckoned, fluid, smooth. Whatever it was could wait. His dreams shifted to summertime—to cookouts with marshmallows and hot dogs on sticks and eyes that stung from campfire smoke.

The flames, no longer content to dance along the paths laid out for them, set out on their own. They ascended, climbed, came together. The roof caved in, and Paul saw the stars. His head hurt. He'd fallen, but he was comfortable now. He smiled in the flickering light.

Chapter 21

Currant snoozed her alarm for the second time and drifted back to sleep. Then the haze from the night before lifted, and her eyes snapped open.

My car.

Two hours and $42 later, Currant set her work bag down on her desk. *I can't believe they charged me the daytime parking rate,* she thought. *I was out by 8:02.* She booted up her computer and went to find some coffee.

The route to the Coffee Bar brought her right past Xander's workstation, but she was tired and asocial and not ready to talk to anyone. *Don't look up don't look up don't look up.*

Xander looked up. "Hey, Currant! Happy Tuesday. Are you going for coffee?"

"Yeah! I was just going to ask if you wanted to come with." She eyed the mug on his desk. "Or have you already been?" she asked hopefully.

"I'm ready for my second cup," Xander said. He locked his computer and jumped up to join her.

"How was the long weekend?" Currant asked.

"Amazing! I picked up a city bike down by Lake Nokomis and rode it all the way up to Bde Maka Ska."

"To what?"

"Bde Maka Ska. You know, the biggest lake in the Chain of Lakes."

"You mean Lake Calhoun?" Currant was puzzled.

"I think that's what it was formerly known as, but the signs all say 'Bde Maka Ska.' That's its original Dakota name."

"Oh," said Currant.

"Yeah, it was really nice. I found this cute little localvore café with *incredible* crêpes, and last night, I matched with someone on Tinder that I think might be my soulmate."

"Not bad for your first weekend in town," Currant said.

"Right?" said Xander. "Minnesota isn't so bad after all."

When they reached the Coffee Bar, Currant looked around for a veteran employee who could make them their drinks, but Xander headed straight for the espresso machine.

"Whoa, where'd you learn to do that?" she asked.

Xander furrowed his brow. "At barista training. I did my In-Store Experience at the Bloomington South store last week. Hasn't your manager signed you up yet?"

No, my manager has not signed me up. My manager is absentee unless he wants to talk bonfire food. "You know, I think he mentioned something about it, but he's been super busy. I'll double-check with him."

Xander said that he would show her a couple of things, and then pulled, tamped, and steamed like a pro. Currant followed along, fumbling her way through her first real cappuccino. She was disproportionately proud of the resulting product. *I made this! A real, tangible, actual thing.* It was a little weak, and the milk was scalded, but all Currant could taste was success.

"So how was your first week?" Xander asked as they headed back toward their wing.

"It was good," Currant said. "Lots of information to absorb."

"Same," Xander said, eyebrows up for emphasis. "But for real, your week was good? No tension in your team? I mean, I know Visual Identity is struggling…"

Currant's eyebrows lowered. "What do you mean, 'struggling'?"

"Nothing! Nothing. It's just that I'm working on a strategic succession positioning plan, you know? And there's a *lot* of discussion about your department."

What does that mean? Are they getting fired? Am I getting fired? Currant's mind churned.

Xander didn't seem to notice. He peeled off when they reached his workstation, and Currant continued pensively toward her desk.

When she got back to the Visual Identity enclave, Gianna and Beck were leaving.

"You coming, baby girl?"

"Where?"

"The Marketing All-Hands Meeting," Beck replied. "It starts in two minutes."

"Oh. It wasn't on my calendar."

Beck shrugged. He and Gianna headed off down the hall, and Currant followed behind them.

When they got to Matterhorn, most of the seats were taken. Beck and Gianna took the last two chairs at the table.

"Oh…," said Beck, as people shifted to make room. "Why don't you go grab a chair from the Coffee Bar?"

Currant did as she was told. The four-top was occupied; the sturdy pine stools from the tall café table were her only option. She grabbed one, lugged it back into the conference room, and put it down in the spot that had been cleared for her. She climbed up, knees level with the tabletop, head two feet above the crowd, and fought hard to believe no one noticed.

"Awesome. Let's get started." Beck cleared his throat. "First off, as CMO, I want to recognize each and every person in this room. Nothing makes a leader happier than knowing he's got a great team beneath him, and you all were absolutely tenacious last quarter. The metrics show it. Engagement across socials is skyrocketing, thanks to the community-building that Ellis has been doing…"

A Warby-Parkered content manager across the table from Currant namasted in thanks.

"… and Crystal has been *relentless* on the customer journey mapping. Twenty-seven touchpoints, isn't that right, Crystal?"

The woman below Currant and to the right nodded.

"Part of my role as CMO is to syndicate best practices, innovation, and cultural change both within and without of the company. I was recently featured on Creatives Today, an industry-leading podcast featuring other CMOs and thought leaders, where I discussed the incredible work that we are doing here at AlChal. Gianna, can you pull it up?"

"What'd you say?" Gianna said, looking over at him.

"Can you pull up the website so we can play the podcast?" He punched the button on the projector in the middle of the conference table and handed the HDMI cable to Gianna.

She plugged it in, and her screen ghosted into view on the wall. "Now where am I going?" she asked.

"It's www.creativestoday.co—no M on the end," Beck answered.

"Cre-a-tives to-day…" Gianna murmured, fingers flat on the keys under long, crimson nails. As she typed, her browser auto-suggested recently visited webpages. Currant recognized one: www.cretincountygazette.com. *Weird*, Currant thought. *That's from up by my cabin.*

Gianna made it to the podcast site and clicked on Beck's picture. "This one? It says it's thirty-eight minutes long."

"Yeah, well, we don't have to listen to the whole thing. Let's just start and see how much we get through."

Thirty-nine minutes later, Currant climbed down from her chair. She picked it up, balancing her empty mug on its golden pine seat, and filed out the door to the conference room with the rest of the marketers.

When she was finally back at her desk, Currant willed herself into work mode. *Week Two at Alpine Chalet Coffee Company*, she thought, turning to a fresh page in her notebook. She wrote **To Accomplish** at the top, underlined it twice, and then drew a trail of checkboxes down the left margin.

Thus organized, she turned to her inbox. At the very top was a message from Beck, sent a few minutes before with High Importance.

`Hey, Currant -`

`If it's at all doable food-safety-wise, can we go with REAL marshmallow sticks for the bonfire? I know you can get stainless steel ones, but wood just has that vibe... The only question mark then is who would whittle them.`

```
Can you check on that? EOD is
fine.

-B-
```

Currant sighed and added **Check on whittlers** as To-Do Number One.

The next few emails were FYI, so she moved them to a subfolder. Then she came to a meeting notice for that evening:

```
LATTE Participant Happy Hour
(Informal) - 5:30pm.
```

Hey :) short notice i know, Jenna had written, **but would be great to get to know each other less formally! hope you can make it**

Currant accepted.

Ten minutes and twenty-seven emails later, she was at Inbox Zero. Then a message popped up from Gwen: **We have a package for you at reception.**

Currant ran down the hall and grabbed the FedEx. Back at her desk, she slit it open, revealing ten stainless-steel double-walled commuter tumblers.

"The test run is here!"

No one heard her; at least, no one looked up. She pulled one of the mugs out of its plastic. The #FuelYourFire campfire design blazed up at her, and her shoulders slumped. *Oh, yeah,* she thought, remembering Paul's business plan. *My logo's stolen.*

But the tumbler looked fine, and she had a job to do. *Art is imitation,* she reminded herself. *This is just how the game is played.*

She fired off an email to the vendor. **The test run looks great,** she typed. **How quick can we get the rest of the order?**

Chapter 22

When she walked into the lobby later that afternoon, Max and Xander were already there. Purnima arrived within seconds, moving fast and checking her phone. "Jenna is going to be late, so she'll just meet us there." She looked at the gathered group. "So we're just waiting on Sung-Min?"

"And Karina," Max said. "I invited her."

Both stragglers showed up as they were speaking, and they caravanned toward the restaurant, Purnima's starter Audi in the lead.

They arrived and were led to a long, tall, butcher-block table. A line of succulents in tiny pots marched down the middle like little green army men; exposed Edison lightbulbs hung from copper arms, casting the group in a modern-vintage glow.

"We have *got* to order the calamari," Xander proclaimed as the waitress distributed menus. "It's so good here."

"And the Cajun Scotch eggs," Purnima added. "They're all small plates—let's just order a bunch and share."

The waitress returned almost instantaneously for their order. No one else ordered beer, so Currant skimmed the list of signature drinks. "I'll do a Maple Bacon Manhattan, please."

Jenna arrived just before the waitress bounded away. She added a Mangotini to the mix, and then cleared her throat.

"Thank you all for being here," she started. "I thought this would be a great way for us to get to know each other outside of work. To begin, I suggest we each share a—"

"Why don't we just chat a bit, instead?" Sung-Min said. "Keep it low-key."

Everyone nodded.

"So what do you all think of AlChal after your first week?" Karina asked.

The six new employees started to answer simultaneously, mouths gaping open like a nest of baby starlings.

"...and don't tell me there's a lot of information to absorb," she continued.

All six mouths slammed shut.

A beat of silence as they regrouped. "It's not what I expected," Purnima said finally.

"Right?" said Xander. "This is nothing like MBA school."

Then the server arrived, setting a full tray of drinks on a folding stand next to their table. Another server brought over a tray of tapas, and the two of them set about distributing glasses and small plates until every square inch of the table was covered.

I need to say something, Currant thought. *I haven't said anything since we got here.* She waited until the flurry of activity had passed, and then raised her Maple Bacon Manhattan. "To Alpine Chalet Coffee Company," she said. "And to playing the game."

"To playing the game," they all echoed.

Even without Jenna's structured icebreaker, the group found things to talk about.

"I mean, does it *really* matter if the Product Sales Dashboard is updated real-time or with a twenty-minute delay?" Purnima said. "My boss showed me the view logs, and no one even accesses it except for the last week of the quarter, but the CIO watched a Tableau webinar last week and now he has all these demands."

"...but then sometimes the stores don't submit their Inventory and Orders Report on time, because there's an afternoon rush or whatever, and then we have to manually override our pick lists and distribution plan, and it takes *forever*." Jenna sounded outraged.

"What's the deal with you and Andrea Pleney?" Max asked Karina. "During the Onboarding session on the first day, it seemed like you two aren't overly fond of each other."

"Andrea Pleney, *MA*," Karina corrected him. "Don't forget her credentials."

"No kidding," said Xander. "I went by her desk yesterday because it's Pam's birthday tomorrow, and she *signed the card* with the MA after her name."

"See?" said Karina. "Anyway, remember how I said that I had worked at an AlChal store during college? During my first week at Headquarters, I was in a meeting where Andrea wanted to revamp the Cabin Crew uniform standards because she thought that encouraging braided pigtails was—and I quote—'demeaning' and 'symptomatic of the overt sexualization of the brand,' and it made AlChal an 'unsafe and unsupportive workplace' for female employees."

"Are you kidding?" Currant asked.

"No," Karina said. "She had a bunch of slides with academic citations and everything. So *I* said, since health regulations require employees with long hair to tie it back anyway, it didn't matter whether it was in a ponytail or a pigtail. I also said that, as a female employee, I would feel *less* safe and *less* supported by a workplace that forbid me from wearing my hair in the manner I felt most comfortable with. The leadership team agreed with me and her proposal got shot down."

"What, so Andrea holds a grudge because you out-argued her one time? That seems a bit unreasonable," said Max.

"No," Karina said. "I think it's because, after that meeting, I wore my hair in pigtails every day for two months."

The second round was served, and conversation flowed; it ebbed as the glasses and tapas plates emptied. The server came over to ask if they wanted a third.

"I should probably get home," Purnima sighed. "I actually need to be up at a decent hour tomorrow."

"Come on," Sung-Min said. "It's not even eight o'clock yet."

"Yeah, but it's a Tuesday."

Currant was up for another drink, but Max and Jenna said they had to leave, too. After a few minutes of check-splitting calculations, the evening came to an end.

"Man, a couple of months ago, the night would just be getting started," said Sung-Min as they walked toward their cars. "You're right, Xander—this is nothing like MBA school."

Chapter 23

The rest of the week passed in a flash of emails and spreadsheets. Currant was settling into the corporate rhythm, making headway on the merchandising selection, and had even found out that one of the guys in Accounting led a troop of Girl Scouts who were eager to earn their Woodworking badge. He had promised 120 whittled sticks by start of business on Monday.

The weekend passed quickly, too. Currant had been so exhausted on Friday evening that she had gone to bed after a single episode of Netflix. Saturday was spent on domestic things: grocery shopping, meal prepping, laundry. On Sunday evening, bored, she opened her work laptop. *I'll just get a couple of emails off my plate so I can hit the ground running tomorrow,* she thought.

Four hours later, Currant tipped her head back and tapped the bottom of the bottle to coax the last bit of IPA foam into her mouth. *FullDayDinInstoreCollatTracker_v2_bonfire.xlsx* was full-screened on her monitor, and she had just marked the very last task as 'Complete'.

I did it. I'm done. My first big project.

She forced herself to smile since she knew rationally that she should, but the excitement was muted. Despite a week of playing Fake-It-Till-You-Make-It with a corporate sense of right and wrong, the knowledge that the #FuelYourFire design was being used dishonestly still prickled her conscience.

It prickled enough to keep her from sleeping, or at least from sleeping well. Currant gave up at 4:30 and got out of bed; she had to be up early anyway. After brewing a cup of coffee, she headed back to the bathroom and stared hard at her reflection.

How big of a deal is it, really, that the logo is stolen? She considered emailing her Corporate Ethics professor to ask his advice, but he had asked her out a couple of times, and she didn't want to send any mixed signals. She sighed and opened Instagram. She searched, found what she was looking for, and then turned back to the mirror.

Currant parted her hair and thought about right and wrong. Was there a universal line? She felt that there was—but did this cross it? And even if so, did she have a responsibility to get involved? She fumbled with a bobby pin. *What would 'getting involved' even mean?*

Her arms were fatiguing. Currant dropped them for a moment and switched to her phone's browser. She typed in **design similarities branding**. Nothing useful. She tried **intellectual property violation similar brand**. Legalese. She typed in **logo is stolen what to do**, got no help from Google, and whimpered. *Why can't anything be easy?*

Currant returned to Instagram and returned to her task. The beauty influencer made it look so simple, but Currant had difficulty keeping up. After a few fits and starts, she secured a perfect French-braided pigtail on the left side of her head.

Am I really sure the design is stolen? She knew that she was, but wanted to confirm. There wasn't much hope that she'd find the logo online—as far as she knew, it existed only in Paul's business plan—but she went back to the browser and typed in **camp out café** anyway.

AREA MAN KILLED IN FIRE.

Currant froze. She clicked the link and was taken to an article in the Cretin County Gazette.

Paul Manter, 53, of Poppel Township, was killed early Tuesday morning in a devastating fire at the Camp Out Café Bar and Grill, which he owned. Firefighters from the Poppel-Greenland Volunteer Fire Cooperative were able to contain the flames before they spread to a pole barn on the property.

The cause of the fire, which appeared to have originated in the front of the restaurant, has not been determined. A person familiar with the investigation reported "traces of accelerant" at the scene.

When asked about the possibility of arson, PGVFC Fire Chief Glen Sorensen responded, "We aren't ruling anything out."

Currant could hear her heart pounding. She stared at the picture of Paul on her phone's tiny screen. He had been so excited about his remodel—big plans, big dreams—and then, suddenly, he was gone.

And his campfire logo was gone, too.

Paul is dead. And if the fire was set intentionally… Currant's mind and fingers raced. The stolen design had shot out from the ethical grey zone into the blood red of arson and murder. *I don't have a choice anymore*, she thought, barely conscious of her braiding. *I can't not get involved*. There was now no question about right or wrong.

She finished her second pigtail and checked it in the mirror. Her reflection confirmed what she already knew: the right side was messier.

Keep it together, Currant. She tugged on her stretch-denim, too-expensive Work Jeans and a fitted heather grey tee and then gathered her things, willing herself to concentrate. She kept focus long enough to make sure her Honda didn't get on the wrong highway, and then loosed her grip on the panic. Her thoughts ricocheted out, bouncing off of one another like negative ions.

I have to call the police.

What am I going to say? "Hi, I'm Currant Keppler, and I'd like to report Alpine Chalet Coffee Company for arson and murder because we have a logo that looks like the dead guy's logo?"

Currant went cold. *Alpine Chalet Coffee Company?* For the first time, Currant realized that the *company* hadn't done anything—a *person* had.

She had been treating the situation like a case study, a set of constraints imposed upon her which she had to navigate through. But this wasn't HBR, and the obstacle in her path wasn't put there by market forces. The invisible hand didn't start fires.

Gianna.

Gianna had presented the new design on Currant's second day of work. Not only that, but she had the Cretin County Gazette website in her browser history.

She must have been looking at the news coverage! Don't arsonists get off on that sort of thing? They always go back to the scene of the crime or collect news clippings in scrapbooks or something.

Currant lifted her phone, but then hesitated once more. *I can't call the police. I'm driving. Plus, why would they believe me? I don't have any evidence.*

She dropped her phone back in her purse and started to plan. She didn't have evidence *yet...* but she would find some.

Chapter 24

But not today. Today, she was headed to Store #743 in Apple Valley for her In-Store Experience. After Xander had asked why her manager hadn't signed her up for her ISE, Currant had rationalized it. *I don't need an in-store experience,* she had thought. *Like Gavin said, I have the most directly applicable experience in the whole group. That's probably why Beck hasn't made it a priority.*

Then an email landed in her inbox with subject line **FW: LATTE Participant ISE Requirement**. Currant had seen that it was an email chain and scrolled to the bottom. The first message, dated a month before, was a courteously worded request to all LATTE project leaders to indicate which day during their new employee's first two weeks of tenure would be best for their In-Store Experience. After that, dated a week later, was a courteously worded follow-up from Karina to Beck, reminding him to fill out the form, and then another, less courteously worded follow-up. Finally, there was a message from Karina indicating that Currant had been assigned an ISE slot at Store #743 the following Monday. That assignment had been sent last Tuesday; Beck had added **happy Sunday, CurranT! fyi** and forwarded it to her the morning before.

The dining room was dark when she arrived, but she could see a warm yellow light glowing from behind the counter. She didn't see anyone, but the door was unlocked, so Currant stepped inside.

The scent of freshly ground coffee, industrial spray cleaner, and mass-produced muffins enveloped her like a hug. A singer-songwriter song, engineered to sound indie, sparkled softly from hidden speakers, and a high-resolution fire crackled warmly from an LED flatscreen.

The manufactured coziness transported Currant back to the sandwich shop she had managed. The sights and sounds had been different, but curated to induce the same welcoming feeling. She remembered quiet mornings baking bread, counting inventory, and filling out shift schedules. *I was good at that job*, she thought, awash in the memory of feeling confident and effective. A sense of calm came over her as she headed toward the counter; she was walking back into her comfort zone.

"Good morning," Currant said to the back of the person in the back room. She had considered herself authorized to breach the Employees Only area, since she was already on Alpine Chalet's payroll.

"Hey," said the woman without turning around. She was perched on a step ladder, reaching up toward an open box of paper cups on the top of an industrial shelving rack. "Currant, right? One second, I'm just trying to..." Her voice dropped. "...twenty-two, twenty-four, twenty-six times sixty..."

"Update the inventory count? I know how that goes. I was a store manager, too, for three—or was it four?—years. Not at AlChal, but somewhere similar. I've probably done twenty-seven million inventory counts in my life... it seems like thirty-five of my fifty-hour week was devoted to trying to figure out how much of everything we had on hand."

"...twenty-seven times fifty... no, wait..."

"No problem, take your time," Currant said. "I'm fifteen minutes early, anyway."

She glanced around the room, taking in the bulletin board above the desk, crowded with official communication from AlChal Headquarters. A memo alerting Cabin Crew Managers and Supervisors to the upcoming Full-Day Dining Initiative rollout caught her eye, but it was more of a Save-the-Date than actual information. *There's nothing there about the logo, thank God.*

"Okay, sorry about that. I'm Leslie."

Currant looked up. The woman walked toward her, hand extended. "Welcome to my store. Let's get you started, shall we?"

"Sure," Currant said, shaking Leslie's hand. "What needs to happen? Do you have a Pre-Open Checklist? Is there Prep to be done? The lobby looked like it was in pretty good shape, but if you want me to take another sweep through with the mop, I'd be happy to. Just let me know what you need, and I'm sure I can figure it out. I may be from Corporate, but I got my start behind the counter."

Leslie looked tired. *That's odd*, Currant thought. *I'd think she'd be used to the early-morning hours by now.*

Leslie put her to work measuring out 25 ounces of Zurich Zip Medium Roast beans into industrial-size coffee filters and then turned the volume up on the store's network of hidden speakers. Currant diligently stacked up ten of the prepared packets, and then ground the first batch and set the giant urn to brew. Opening time was approaching.

At 5:57, Leslie dialed back the music, and at 5:58, the first customer arrived. "Hi! Welcome to Alpine Chalet Coffee Company," Currant chirped from behind the bakery case. "What can I get for you?"

The customer looked surprised. "Um," she said, looking from Currant to Leslie, who had come up behind Currant, carrying a paper cup. "It's a medium skim latte with an extra shot," Leslie said, ringing the drink up. "Here you go, Manda." Manda touched a debit card to the contactless payment terminal, murmured what might have been a "Thank you," and was out the door by 5:59.

The next person through the door was in a hurry. "Hi," Currant said. "Welcome to Al– "

"Hey, Leslie," he said, sliding behind the counter. "Hi. I'm Quint," he said to Currant. Currant shook his hand, and Quint went to the storage room, came back with an apron, and then took up his spot at the espresso machine.

"You just shadow Quint," Leslie said. "He'll show you everything you need to know."

Currant spent a blissful, pigtailed day behind the counter, losing herself in the rhythm of the work. Quint had shown her how to steam milk and pull espresso shots, and then had stationed her at the blender with a ring-bound binder of laminated recipe cards when business picked up. Currant made Avalanccinos like she'd been born doing so, chatting naturally with customers as she handed over Swiss Chocolate Cherry Blossoms and Marshmallow Mocha Mountaintops. *I am really, really good at this.* She worked through her lunch break and was disappointed when Leslie told her that her shift was over.

"Are you sure? I don't mind staying longer. I'm salaried, so it won't cost you any overtime." Leslie said she was sure.

Currant went to the back room, untied her apron, and put it in the laundry hamper. She grabbed her purse and the half-drunk Frozen Hot Apple Cider that she had made for herself during the afternoon lull, and then walked out into the grey, threatening heat. As the door shut behind her, it started to rain, and with the first flash of lightning, Currant's anxiety returned. *I work with a murderer.*

Chapter 25

When Currant arrived at the office the next morning, Gianna was already there.

"Hey, baby girl," she said.

"Good morning, Gianna," Currant said carefully. She wasn't scared, exactly; in her lime green twin set and faux leather pants, Gianna didn't seem very threatening. *But I know what she's capable of.*

She thought she knew, at least; she still needed to find proof, some evidence that linked Gianna to the Camp Out Café. Currant had never investigated anything before, but she had watched some tutorials on YouTube and felt confident in her ability.

But that would come later—she had work to do first. Jenna had scheduled an "emergency"

Pitch Contest Prep session first thing that morning, so Currant grabbed her laptop and headed for the meeting room.

"We're behind schedule."

Jenna projected her screen on the wall and stared accusingly around the table. "I wanted to start on my task last week, but I couldn't, because the predecessor task wasn't done."

She circled the cursor over the offending section of the Gantt chart and glared at Xander.

"What are we looking at?" asked Max.

Jenna ignored him. "The entire refreshment procurement process is on hold until I know how many participants and judges I need to provide for," she said. "Xander, you were supposed to get that information to me two days ago."

"We'll have five finalists. I told you that."

"I need to know how many *judges*, Xander. They're the ones we have to impress. They're the ones who should be established in their fields and thus have meaningful social media followings. I've optimized the entire catering concept for aesthetics to harness what should be sizeable Instagram play."

"I'm working on it," Xander said. "We are only partnering with leaders from the fastest-growing start-ups, so by definition, they are too busy to respond to emails right away. I've got four confirmed judges, and I'm just waiting on the last two."

"Well, follow up. I need those numbers— I'm completely blocked until you do your job."

"Why don't you go ahead and order based on the assumption that we'll have the full panel?" asked Currant. "You could always caveat it with the fact that there might be a slight reduction if the last two judges can't make it."

"I'm not going to *guess*, Currant. We're dealing with perishable inventory here. If I order too much, we end up with food waste, which directly contradicts our corporate shared value of sustainability, and if I don't order enough, we can't fulfill our brand promise of nourishing customers throughout their day." Jenna's voice started to shake. "Plus, we need to discern coffee preferences, degrees of veganism… there are still so many unknowns!"

"Hey, hey, okay." Xander reached toward Jenna and patted her hand. "I'll DM the last two judges again this afternoon."

Purnima spoke up. "Have we decided on the final list of nominees? We're going to want to highlight each finalist and their start-up idea on our socials to build traction before the event, so we need to get posting."

"Yes, we have," Xander answered. "Drum roll, please." He unplugged the HDMI cable from Jenna's laptop and plugged it into his. A minimalist presentation materialized on the wall, the words **Fuel Your Fire** in 100-point font ringed by five tiny oval-cropped photos with barely legible text.

"First, let me tell you a little about my process. I reviewed more than thirty multimedia business plans, and then spoke personally to ten promising candidates. I was able to narrow the field to the five finalists you see here."

"We *can't* see them," said Sung-Min. "They're too small."

Xander clicked smugly, and the screen zoomed in tight on one oval. "This is Victoria Okoye," he said. He clicked again, and the screen panned way out and then way back in on blue-green script reading *Grounds4Life*. "Grounds4Life connects coffee shops with urban gardeners who use the coffee grounds for organic, chem-free growing."

Another click, another too-fast zoom across the presentation template to the next pitch contest finalist. "Adeel Siddiq…"

Currant closed her eyes in anticipation of the jump.

"…created BlockBox, which is a really promising early-stage competitor for Google Docs, but adds the security of the blockchain to your Track Changes."

Xander clicked again.

"What is this program?" asked Max.

"It's Prezi," Xander answered. "PowerPoint is so boring, right? So *Microsoft*. I thought I'd change things up."

"It's giving me vertigo."

Currant laughed, but Max actually looked green.

Xander exited Presentation mode and flipped ahead statically to the next finalist. Madison Johnsen's company, Lentilix, used optical character recognition and real-time image info to highlight vegan and vegetarian options on printed menus. Then came Alex Lee with St*rlght, a content management app that could snip text, audio, and images from TikTok for simultaneous cross-media posting to other platforms.

Currant had been checking her email, but her attention snapped back to the screen when Xander clicked forward to the final nominee. *He made it!*

"This is Luke Kennedy from Regulr."

I should probably tell them I'm dating him, she thought, cheeks flushing with pride. *I'm sure there's no conflict of interest, but...*

Currant cleared her throat. "Guys, in the interest of disclosure, I should tell you that I know Luke Kennedy. In fact—"

"So does Xander," said Purnima.

Current noticed *his* cheeks going pink.

"What's that all about?" Max asked, picking up on Purnima's tone.

"Well," Xander said, "It's crazy how small-world Minneapolis is. I happen to know Lucas, um, *socially*, as well as professionally."

"Socially?" Purnima threw in. "Is that what we're calling it?"

Xander's cheeks deepened to full-on fire-engine red. "I can assure you, there's no conflict of interest."

Luke and Xander? But how could that be?

She thought back to Memorial Day evening; she hadn't been misreading the signs—she *knew* she hadn't. His hand on her thigh, that last kiss before he left to solve his work crisis… *I mean, next time, we'll definitely…*

Leaden realization settled over her like an x-ray smock at the dentist's office; 'next time' should have happened by now. She hadn't heard from Luke in almost a week.

Luckily, there wasn't much Pitch Contest prep left to discuss. Jenna ended the meeting with a perfunctory "Great work, guys!" and Currant beelined for the door. *I knew it was too good to be true*, she thought. *Why would someone like Luke Kennedy be interested in me?*

She held it together until she reached the restroom; there, in the safety of a stall, she crumpled. The tears came up fast, breaching their bounds, but crested fairly quickly. Then she straightened, opened the door, and checked her reflection in the bathroom mirror. *Two weeks ago, I cried for, like, ten minutes. This is already significant progress.* She dabbed at her eyes and headed back toward her desk.

It hit her halfway down the hallway. Luke hadn't just ghosted her—he'd ghosted her for Xander.

Her colleague.

In charge of selecting finalists for the Pitch Contest.

Minneapolis is small, but it's not that small, she thought. Her eyes narrowed and she went to find Sung-Min.

Currant had a plan.

Chapter 26

On the way home that evening, emotionally whiplashed and nursing her heartbreak, Currant slapped the steering wheel. *Shit. I was going to investigate Gianna.* She thought about turning around, but badging in at this time of night would leave a trail. She sighed, slipping across lanes to get to her exit. *I'll do it tomorrow.*

She did it on Thursday. Wednesday filled itself with back-to-back meetings, and Currant had to skip lunch; by the time 6:00 PM rolled around, she was starving and went home to eat dinner. But on Thursday afternoon, when Currant finished her last meeting, she strode resolvedly toward her desk. *Tonight's the night*, she thought, a shot of adrenaline coursing through her. *It's now or never.*

Gianna's chair was empty. Beck, however, was at his desk with headphones on, a work-in-progress PowerPoint on one monitor and a video call active on the other. He was looking at his phone.

Currant sat down at her computer and settled in to wait.

"Whoa, you're still here?" It was 6:45 and Beck was just shutting down his laptop.

I've been sitting right behind you for the last two hours, she thought.

Currant smiled sweetly. "Just want to finish up the deck for the employee pre-launch."

"That can wait till tomorrow. There's no rush," he said. "Seriously—go home."

Currant thought fast. "I'm meeting some friends for drinks in Uptown later, so it doesn't make sense to go home first. I'll just do a couple more slides and then head out."

"Yeah? Where are you going?"

"Um… " Currant scrambled to remember the name of a restaurant. "We don't know yet."

"I went to the F. Scott Cigar Bar last night; Eleanor from Controlling recommended it. It's all dark wood and leather—super legit. It's non-smoking, of course, but they have tobacco-scented diffusers."

"Okay, cool," Currant said. "Maybe I'll see if they want to go there."

Beck seemed satisfied with that and bid her good night. She worked for another ten minutes and then took her empty coffee mug on a reconnaissance tour to see who was left in the office. No one.

She placed the mug in the kitchenette's dishwasher and turned back toward her desk, the ponderous silence enveloping her. *Here we go.* As she walked, she reviewed her game plan: try to social-engineer Gianna's password by looking through her file cabinet for hints at her personality.

Currant's fear turned physiological as she reentered the Visual Identity enclave. Her heart pounded, her vision tunneled, and her hands felt like ice. *I'm about to break and enter,* she thought. *I'll be committing a crime.* She took one last look around the empty open office area and crept silently toward Gianna's desk.

She lowered herself into Gianna's chair. *Last chance. I can still turn back. I can pick up my purse and go out to my car and forget I ever heard of the Camp Out Café.* But Currant knew she couldn't forget. A man was dead. She *had* to investigate. She took a deep, ragged breath, let it out slowly, and punched Gianna's spacebar to wake the computer.

The lights went out.

Currant yelped, but recovered quickly. *The office lights must go out at seven*, she thought. It didn't matter; the northern summer sun was reluctant to set, and the floor-to-ceiling window behind the desk let in plenty of light.

She started with the obvious. When she had received her work-issued laptop, her initial password had been **ckeppler1**; she had been forced to change it after the first log-in, but tried **gplatinum1** anyway. No luck. She glanced quickly around, but Gianna's work surface was spotless; no photos, no knickknacks, no post-its with pets' names. She tried **gianna**, **gianna!**, **platinum**, and **password**. Nothing.

She wasn't worried about getting locked out; she had practiced with her own credentials on Monday night, and didn't get a warning message until she had mistyped her password seventeen times. Currant moved on to Phase Two of her plan.

Bending low, she checked the file cabinet under Gianna's desk. It was locked. *Showtime!* She reached in her pocket and produced two pre-straightened bobby pins, then opened her phone to the WikiHow article on lockpicking.

The first pin slipped in smoothly, and she held it down to maintain tension. She put the next bobby pin in, angled just slightly up, and thrilled as her fingers sensed the tumblers rise. The bottom pin turned, and the lock was free. She slid the file drawer open.

The shallow top drawer contained two tubes of lipstick, a wooden train whistle, and a jumble of paperclips, dimes, and binder clips. *A whistle? Weird.* Currant straightened up, typed in **whistle**, **lluvwhistles**, and **whistlewhileuwork**, but the laptop stayed locked.

What am I doing? There's no way I'll be able to guess her password — there are a million possibilities. Currant slumped back in the chair. *Even more if she used special characters.* She made one last attempt, **i<3whistles**, and leaned down with a sigh to push the drawer back in.

The momentum of the push caused one of the file folders to gape open, and Currant's eyes went wide. She reached in, spreading the folder further with her fingers, and there, on a crumpled corner ripped off from a larger sheet, was the campfire design. The sketch was rough, harsh scratches with a blue ballpoint pen, but there was no mistaking it. Currant flipped the scrap over to find half of a Fish Finder Puzzle and an ad for Thousand Lakes Savings & Loan. *The placemat.*

Gotcha, she thought.

The click of the lights sounded like a rifle report. Currant shoved the drawer closed and looked down the wing. The first bank of ceiling lights, closest to the lobby, blazed like the headlights of an oncoming car.

Those are motion-activated. She sat frozen, dazed, for a second or two… and then the next set of lights clicked on.

With the sound of her blood pounding in her ears, Currant scanned the area for available cover. *The Marketini Lounge.* She crouch-ran soundlessly to the shamrock green love seat, hit the floor, and rolled underneath.

Maybe someone forgot something. Or maybe it's the cleaning crew. Currant prayed for the sound of a vacuum. Instead, she heard footsteps… and they were coming right toward her.

Chapter 27

Currant held her breath as the footsteps approached. From her green-velvet vantage point, she saw a pair of well-worn-in Red Wings, moving purposefully in a long, heavy gait. They passed quickly and turned into the Visual Identity enclave.

That can't be Beck—his boots are brand-new and his legs aren't that long.

The footsteps moved toward the far end of the row. *Oh shit oh shit oh shit*, Currant thought. *Did I close the file cabinet?*

The jingle of keys, a soft metallic slide, and a hushed shuffle of paper. Then the thunk of a drawer, a lock ratcheting closed, and the heavy boots approached again.

They turned away from her and retreated down the hallway. When they faded, she scrambled, less gracefully than she'd have liked, out from under the couch. She ran over to Gianna's desk, pulling her bobby pins out as she went. *Please, please, please*, she thought, as she coaxed the lock open.

An engine started in the parking lot, and she jerked her head toward the window behind her. A black Toyota pickup truck turned on its headlights and rolled across the blacktop.

The tumblers clicked and Currant yanked the drawer open.

The folder was gone.

She grabbed her bag, wrenched her laptop from its docking station, and sprinted outside. She had parked in the far corner of the lot that morning, anticipating her late exit and not wanting her car to be alone and conspicuous in the middle of the lot. She threw herself behind the wheel and took off after the Toyota.

Fueled by adrenaline, Currant hurtled through the office park. As someone who rarely exceeded the speed limit by more than 10%, the chase was exhilarating. She stomped the brakes once for a squirrel, but otherwise kept her foot to the floor.

Taillights appeared as she crested the last rise in the road; her quarry was waiting at the stoplight. She saw the light turn green, still a hundred yards out, and the black Toyota turned onto the on-ramp for Highway 169 South.

I have to make that light or I'll never find him on the highway. Currant pushed her little Honda harder.

She slid through the intersection as the light changed from yellow to red.

Traffic was thin this late in the evening, and Currant caught up to the truck easily. She followed at a reasonable distance, letting other cars cut in and out between her and her target. Her breathing returned to normal as her cortisol levels settled, and the logical part of her brain regained control. *What am I going to do now?*

She didn't have much time to strategize; two cars ahead, the Toyota turned on its blinker and merged onto the exit. A Hyundai Sonata followed the truck up the ramp, and Currant followed the Sonata. At the top of the ramp, the pickup turned right and the Sonata turned left. Currant was now directly in pursuit.

There were several big intersections on this stretch of road, and Currant panicked when the first light turned red. *Will he see me in his rearview mirror?* She stopped well behind the truck and leaned way over onto the passenger side, pretending to rummage in her purse. The light turned green, Currant popped back into view, and off they went.

For about thirty seconds. They hit another red light, and then another one after that. *Stupid traffic planners!* At the third intersection, the light was quick; Currant didn't have time to hide. From her upright position, she could read the white plastic frame around the truck's license plate: **My other car is a model railroad**.

The strip malls and gas stations died down, and they entered a quieter residential neighborhood. Townhouses turned to single-families, and Starbucks turned to supper clubs. The pickup slowed and turned into the entrance of Andy's Bar and Grille.

Currant kept going. She took the next right turn, and the next after that. She pulled to the curb by a brown split-level with all-weather siding and considered her options. The person in the pickup had taken the sketch of the stolen logo from Gianna's desk. He was currently in Andy's Bar and Grille, a public place with witnesses inside, judging from the cars in the parking lot, and Currant needed to know what he knew.

I already followed him to the suburbs, she thought. *Might as well finish the job.* She pulled away from the curb, took two more rights, and then pulled into the parking lot of Andy's Bar and Grille.

Andy's was smaller than it looked from the outside. Currant pushed open the door and almost ran into the bar. A few tall, built-in booths lined the left wall, and a miniature locomotive on a custom-built shelf chugged doggedly around the room.

Currant entered uncertainly. There were five or six people scattered throughout, and she realized that she didn't know who she was looking for. *Unless he's carrying a file folder under his arm, I'm not going to recognize him. I only saw his boots.*

His boots! Currant started scanning footwear. No Red Wings. She couldn't see under the tables of the booths, but the only one occupied held a couple in their seventies.

"Get you something?" The bartender wiped his hands on a towel and walked toward Currant.

I can't just leave; that would be weird, Currant thought. She ordered a Schell's Dark and took an empty bar stool.

She was stumped. The truck was in the parking lot, but there were no beat-up work boots in the entire bar. *Did he know I was following him? Maybe he changed his shoes to throw me off the trail.* Currant took another look around. She studied the faces of the people at the bar, wondering which one of them she had pursued here. Only then did she notice the half-empty beer glass at the seat next to her.

Time slowed. *There's someone in the bar that I haven't seen.* Her brain registered the sound of a door opening and closing. She was turning on her barstool, looking for the bathrooms, when a heavy hand clapped down on her shoulder. His breath was hot on her ear and his whisper was harsh:

"You shouldn't be here, Currant."

Chapter 28

What do I do? Should I scream?

She was about to scream. Then he said, "Put her beer on my tab, Andy. We're moving to that booth over there."

Currant stopped. She knew that voice.

"Sure thing, Silverman," the bartender said.

"Gianna?"

Currant stared across the table. The person staring back at her had on a charcoal grey Henley and a Minnesota Twins cap; this was not the platinum-wigged bombshell that Currant saw every day at work.

"Call me John," he said. "What are you doing here? What do you want?"

His brown eyes were large even without the frame of fake lashes, and they looked worried. He took off his hat and ran a hand over short salt-and-pepper hair.

I don't actually know what I'm doing here. Currant's hands were clasped tight around her pint glass, and she raised it to her lips to buy time for a response.

She sat the beer down. "I know all about it, Gianna."

"It's *John*, Currant, and I know you know all about it, because you're sitting here in front of me," John snapped. "You caught me. Congratulations."

Oh, thought Currant. *I was not expecting that*. It was a little anticlimactic. "Well, why'd you do it?"

John sighed. "I'm good at my job, Currant. I've been a marketer for twenty years. My position was at risk, and I wasn't going to sit back and let it all go up in smoke."

Was that an arson pun? Does he think this is a joke?

"There are other ways to keep a job," she said.

"Yeah, well, I didn't see any other options open to me at the time." He picked at the label on his beer bottle. "And it's not that big a deal, is it? It's a side of me, maybe not one I'd prefer to display all the time, but I'm not ashamed of it."

Not ashamed? Currant was speechless. *He is a psychopath.*

John was silent for a moment. "How did you find out?"

"You read the Cretin County Gazette. I saw it auto-complete in your browser bar when you were pulling up Beck's podcast at the All-Hands meeting. And I found the sketch in your file cabinet."

"You *what*? Why were you in my file cabinet?" John narrowed his eyes. "You were in the office just now, weren't you? That's why my drawer wasn't locked."

"I was under the couch. I heard you coming in, so I hid."

"Good for you for fitting—that couch sits low." John looked down at his hands, sighed again. "I knew I'd get caught sooner or later, but at least I had a pretty good run."

A good run? How many more people has he murdered?

233

He smiled ruefully. "Plus, didn't I tell you that sometimes you have to do whatever it takes to succeed?"

Currant gaped at him. "Well, yeah, John, I didn't think you meant killing people!"

John's smile snapped off. "What are you talking about, Currant?"

"I'm talking about Paul Manter, the owner of the Camp Out Café! I'm talking about the man that you killed in the fire that you started just so you could steal a stupid logo! I'm talking about *murder*!"

A shudder coursed through her, and her voice broke. Saying the word "murder" made it real. *This isn't just some detective game.*

"I didn't murder anyone, Currant. I didn't set anything on fire. And I didn't steal any..." John sat back, realization flooding his face. "You mean the Lunch Launch logo?"

"Yes, I mean the Lunch Launch logo. What else would I mean?"

"Nothing. But I didn't come up with that logo."

"What? Then who did?"

"Beck. He brought it to me a couple weeks ago and asked me to 'see if I could do anything with it'. He's brought me ideas before, and they were nothing like this, but I thought maybe he had just been warming up. The design was good, and we needed a win, so I polished it a little and we ran with it."

Currant rubbed her temple. *Beck...?*

"What is this fire you're talking about?" John continued. "Someone got killed?"

She told him about the Camp Out Café, about the arson reported in the Cretin County Gazette, and about Paul Manter and his business plan.

"And you assumed I murdered him." John crossed his arms and fixed Currant in a glare. She saw a bit of Gianna peeking through.

"Well, yeah. I saw the sketch. And you went back to the office after-hours to remove the evidence! I know you took the file folder with you."

"Yes, I went back for a file folder. I had some of my own drawings in there, and I wanted to work on them tonight."

"Okay, but the Cretin County Gazette," she continued. "Why would someone like you — like Gianna — be reading a tiny little newspaper from way upstate?"

"Because I was in it." John looked out from under the bill of his Twins cap, a hint of pride at the corner of his mouth. "I won an award. For my models." He pulled out his phone and showed Currant a bookmarked article: **John Silverman Takes Home Gold at Toy Soldier and Model Railroad Museum's Annual Model Contest.**

"Congratulations," Currant said automatically.

"Thank you. That's why I went back to the office," he added. "I'm starting on a new build—the Rhaetian Railway's Landwasser Viaduct in eastern Switzerland. I left my sketches at work."

Then why was he so defensive earlier? "Then why were you so defensive earlier? What did you think I had caught you at?"

"Well… at being Gianna."

"Oh. Yeah."

"Sure, I'd love to wear khakis every now and then," John explained. "But four years ago, HR made a policy that said all positions at Level 5 and above required a Bachelor's. I have an Associate's degree in Drafting. Never mind the nearly two decades of work I've done since then—they said I either needed to go back to school or get bumped down to Marketing Coordinator." He took a sip of beer. "I had been moonlighting as Gianna for about six months at that point, so I came in the following Monday with my hair and my heels. HR seemed a lot more hesitant to demote Gianna than John."

"That's horrible," Currant said. "You shouldn't be forced to hide who you are just to keep your job. It's well-documented in the literature that encouraging team members to be their authentic selves at work is beneficial for both employees *and* employers."

John shrugged. "Like I said, you do what it takes." He finished his beer, put the bottle on the table. "And Currant? *No one* is their authentic self at work."

Chapter 29

"So it's Beck?" Currant still couldn't believe it.

"It has to be. He brought me the logo. Said it came to him during the corporate fishing trip."

"That's right—he told me that he was up at some lake near my cabin. He must have stopped at the Camp Out Café on the way home, just like I did. Poor Paul must have showed him his business plan… and then Beck must have…" She trailed off.

John shook his head, unbelieving. "I just really can't picture him killing anyone."

"I know," said Currant, swirling the beer in her glass. "He drives a Nissan Leaf."

"But you could picture *me* killing someone, evidently." John's tone shifted abruptly. "What was your plan in coming here, Currant?"

Currant looked down, not meeting his eye. "I—I'm not really sure."

"Damn right you're not sure. You think I murdered someone, so you jump in your car, drive halfway across the metropolitan area, and confront me about it? That seems a little ill-advised."

"Well, I didn't know you were *you*, first of all. And we're in a restaurant. There are witnesses."

"You thought I burned down a restaurant— with someone inside. Maybe think things through a little bit next time."

I guess, looking back on it, it was a little rash. "Yeah, okay."

They sat in silence for a second. "So what do we do now?" Currant asked. "Do we call the police?"

"Uh-uh. There's no 'we'. If *you* want to report this, go ahead, but I want no part of it. I'll give you the sketch, but I'm not getting involved. Plus, I'm on vacation next week."

"So do *I* call the police?"

"What are the police going to do?" said John. "If you're going to tell anyone, tell the company."

Currant drove back home from the suburbs on autopilot. *I need to report this.* Her mind flashed back to onboarding and to Andrea Pleney, MA's SharePoint site. *But that wouldn't be anonymous,* she remembered.

Suddenly, as if in a vision, she saw the Alpine Chalet Coffee Company logo burning through the darkness. It was Store #4, one of the oldest locations in the chain, and the first one to feature an in-store roaster. It had another nostalgic feature, as well, which interested Currant even more.

The store was empty. *What time is it? Are they closed?* The clock above the espresso machine read 9:41. She still had twenty minutes.

The lone employee came out from the back, rolling his red-gingham sleeves up over thick, tattooed forearms. *Wow,* thought Currant, and her eyes widened. *Not my type, but wow.*

241

"Hey," the barista smiled. "What can I get for you?"

Currant ordered a small dark roast. His arm muscles, covered in teal and purple ink, danced as he poured it.

"I love your sleeves," Currant said. "I always thought paisley was for ties or bedspreads, but it looks super cool."

"Thanks," the barista said, and he winked.

Flustered, Currant almost forgot her purpose. She stopped halfway to the door and turned around. The barista noticed her and came back toward the cash register. She smiled apologetically and pointed to the far corner of the dining room to where the ancient, public-use computer sat.

I can't use the Ethics portal, but I can email Andrea directly. Currant opened up a browser window and typed in **tenminuteemail.com**. It was bookmarked. She clicked to the website, activating a temporary, untraceable email address, and watched as the timer started counting down.

An empty Compose Message box loomed before her. *What do I say?* She had to hurry.

To Whom It May Concern: I would like to report that Beck Baker, CMO, stole the logo that will shortly be released as part of the marketing efforts for the Full-Day Dining Initiative; in doing so, I believe he may have committed arson and murder.

She went to the Cretin County Gazette, found the article about the fire, and copied the link into the email.

www.cretincountygazette.com/ arti/42245/campout-fire-arson - Check the logo on the Camp Out Café remodel plan.

She moved the mouse to the send button, but hesitated.

The door chime dinged. A pair of teenagers came in, laughing and carrying skateboards. Currant was still staring at the screen when they left five minutes later with their Swiss Cocoa Chai Lattes. A bright red message bar flashed at the top of the window, warning her that the email address would expire in one minute.

An anonymous email? Really? Only a few people in the entire company knew about the design, so it wouldn't take long to figure out who sent it. *And is that really the type of person I want to be?*

"Want one for the road?"

"What?"

The barista was leaning across the counter on his strong, sexy forearms. "We're closing now, and I'm about to dump the dark roast. Do you want a refill before you head out?"

Currant shook her head. "Thanks, but I have to work in the morning."

"Where do you work?"

"At AlChal, actually. At Headquarters."

The barista lowered his voice. "Are you a spy?"

Currant looked down at the computer screen. The timer on her ten-minute email clicked from 0:03 to 0:02 to 0:01. She watched the countdown end and her message self-destruct. "No," she answered. "No, I'm not."

"Well, I better be extra friendly anyway. What's your name, Valued Customer? I'm Toby."

"I'm Currant," Currant said, approaching the counter. She extended her hand and Toby shook it. "...and, on second thought, sure, I'll take a refill."

Currant got back in her car. *Bias for action,* she thought. She grabbed her phone, turned on the hot spot, opened up her work laptop, and sent Andrea Pleney a non-anonymous email. Then she drove home slowly, sipping her second coffee. *I'm not going to be able to sleep tonight anyway.*

Chapter 30

She *did* sleep, a bit; when the alarm buzzed the next morning, it jolted her out of an anxiety dream. The dread followed her out of bed, lingering, low-grade. It held on till she reached the office.

Neither Beck nor Gianna were at their desks, and Currant said a silent prayer of thanks. She didn't want to talk to anyone, she didn't want to think about anything, she didn't want to work. *I don't have the emotional capacity,* she thought.

Andrea responded mid-morning.

```
Dear Currant,

Thank you for your email. I am
free at 11:30, please stop by if
you can.
```

Kind regards,

Andrea Pleney, MA, she/her/hers

It's 11:32 now. Currant jumped up from her desk.

The door was open; Currant knocked on it anyway. "Hey, Andrea, is now a good time?"

Andrea Pleney, MA, looked up from her computer screen and gave a curt nod. Currant came in, noting the décor—*When was this last remodeled? 1987?*—and shut the door behind her. She took a seat in a mauve-upholstered chair, and waited for Andrea's acknowledgement.

"Just let me finish this sentence," Andrea said, typing. A good three paragraphs later, she pushed herself back from the keyboard and looked toward Currant. "What would you like to speak to me about?"

Currant took a long, steadying breath. She had laid out her discovery in bullet points that morning so that she could remain objective and structured, and recited them now. It didn't take nearly as long as she thought it would.

"… and so, I believe the matter should be looked into, and that Alpine Chalet Coffee

Company should hold off on using the design created for the Full-Day Dining Initiative until the investigation has been completed." She finished speaking and felt instantly unburdened.

"Currant," Andrea said. "Let me tell you what I'm hearing."

She looked tenderly at Currant. "I'm hearing an empowered, educated woman encountering adversity for the first time. I'm hearing a fierce female who has never allowed the world to hold her back finding herself in a position that she can't handle on her own. I'm hearing a strong woman—and you are *so strong*, Currant, don't ever doubt that—facing the harsh realities of this world we live in... and trying to make sense of it by crafting a narrative."

What is she talking about?

"But you don't need to make up stories to be taken seriously. In fact, in some cases, it may actually do more harm than good." Andrea stretched out her hands, palms facing up, to indicate openness. "Tell me what's *really* going on with Beck. Is he discriminating against you? Belittling you? Making you feel like you have nothing to contribute?"

"What? No. He committed a crime."

"Arson and murder, Currant? Forgive me, but that seems a little far-fetched."

"Maybe so, Andrea, but I think it needs to be looked into. If AlChal doesn't think so, then I can go to the police."

"No, no, that won't be necessary," Andrea sighed. "I'll mention it to our legal team and HR." She sat back in her chair and looked coldly at Currant. "Thank you for bringing this to our attention. We'll begin the workplace investigation process and will let you know if we require any more information. In the meantime, you are not to speak to any of your colleagues about it."

"Of course." Currant stood up to leave.

"Are you *sure* you want to do this, Currant? Nobody likes a troublemaker, and we at AlChal are committed to maintaining a positive, trust-based culture. Even when it means we have to make difficult decisions about team fit."

"Yes, Andrea," Currant said. "I'm sure."

Currant couldn't go back to her desk. She checked the time on her phone: 11:41. *It's a little early for lunch, but not unreasonable.* The path to the lobby took her past Accounting, so she veered toward Sung-Min's cubicle.

His boss was with him. Eleanor Banks was perched on his desk, one red-soled Louboutin curled up under her. She was leaning across him to point to something on his monitor, and a bit of lace-topped thigh-high stocking peeked out from under her staid black skirt.

"Oh, sorry," Currant mumbled.

Sung-Min jerked around at the interruption; Eleanor straightened unhurriedly and smoothed her skirt. She looked Currant over, eyes sweeping down to the floor and most of the way back. "Well, hello, there. Sung-Min, who's your friend?"

Ugh, Currant thought. *My eyes are up here.*

"This is Currant," he answered. "She's in the LATTE Program with me."

"Mmm. It's a pleasure to meet you." She motioned back toward the monitor. "Sung-Min, we'll go over this later. In-depth." She swept out of the cubicle, passing very close to Currant, a hint of Chanel trailing behind her.

"Want to get some lunch? I know it's kind of early," Currant asked.

"Sure, Currant. What's up?" He had picked up on the urgency in her voice.

"Nothing, really. I don't know," she said. "Can you drive? I don't have my keys."

"Seriously, Currant, what's going on?"

"I'm not supposed to talk about it," she said, swinging up into Sung-Min's maroon Wrangler Sport.

They pulled out of the parking lot, and the words tumbled out. She told him about her trip up North, about meeting Paul Manter and seeing his logo. She told him about suspecting Gianna and searching her desk for evidence. She glossed over the scene at Andy's Bar and Grille, but told him about finding out that it was Beck. She told him about reporting it all to Andrea Pleney, MA, and not knowing what to do next.

Her monologue lasted the entire drive. Sung-Min pulled in to a strip mall, parking right in the middle of the back of the lot. He turned the car off, and Currant stopped talking, pushing back against the headrest, worn out. She turned to look at Sung-Min.

"Wow," he said. "That's insane." And then, "Where do you want to eat?"

They opted for the restaurant where Currant had eaten with Beck.

"I came here with Beck once," she told Sung-Min when they were seated. "I didn't know he was a murderer then."

Sung-Min took a bite of his Grass-Fed Buffalo Meatloaf. "That is so crazy. I can't believe he killed someone."

"Tell me about it. He's my boss."

"Yeah, and he drives a Nissan Leaf." Sung-Min reached for the ketchup. "But, hey, on the bright side, your plan worked. It had to go through Gavin, but we got the go-ahead."

What plan? Currant had no idea what he was talking about.

"Eleanor loved it. She said that, assuming usage velocity close to our typical frequency metrics, we'd be able to split the expense across at least two fiscal years."

Oh, yeah, that plan. Seems like forever ago. "Did you tell her it was my idea?"

Sung-Min looked sheepish.

"No big deal," she said. "But you owe me."

They finished eating and drove back in silence. When they reached the office lot, Currant sighed. "Thanks, Sung-Min. I needed this. It feels good to finally tell someone." She leaned back in the seat. "I'm emotionally exhausted. Can you drop me by my car? I think I'll just work the rest of the day from home."

Sung-Min looked at her, eyes wide. "Currant, you can't. The Pitch Contest is today. We're already late."

Chapter 31

The Pitch Contest was planned for 2:00 PM, and preparations were due to start at noon. Sung-Min and Currant rolled in at 12:17, and Jenna was in a panic.

"Where were you?" she demanded.

Currant scowled, but Sung-Min stayed calm. "Grabbing lunch," he said. "We're here now."

"Finally. Listen, we've got some headwinds. Xander isn't going to make it, which means we have to redeploy all of his tasks."

"What's wrong with him?" Sung-Min asked.

"He's taking sick-leave PTO," Jenna said. "Some GI thing." Behind her, Purnima mouthed the word 'breakup'.

"I'll take over the Judge's green room because that's has to be done right," Jenna continued. "Max, I need you to manage the Pitcher's green room."

"Hold on a second. I have the IT and sound logistics. Plus, I need to MC." Max looked around the room. "Currant, how much more marketing do you need to do? Can you take green room duty?"

Inwardly, Currant whimpered. *All I want to do is go home.* "Absolutely," she said. "I'll just need Purnima to take care of live-tweeting."

"That's fine," Purnima said. "I've done all my other tasks."

"Great," Jenna said. "Then let's get moving. And remember, guys, this needs to be *perfect*. Currant, go get your green room set up."

The room *was* set up. Matterhorn, the nicest space, had been reserved for the judges, so Currant would be welcoming pitch contestants to the Swiss Army Knife meeting room.

The conference table was shaped like a blade and already covered with food and drink. There were airpots of coffee, thermoses of milk, bottles of water, and pitchers of tea. Scones, muffins, cookies, and bars filled round plastic trays, and cups, plates, and napkins were arranged on the credenza. A side table had been set up with the new sandwich oven. Its shovel stood gleaming and ready.

Karina walked in with a green plastic crate. "Hey, Currant. You manning the oven?"

"Evidently," she said. *Good thing I got my MBA.*

Karina had barely unloaded the sandwiches from the crate when the first pitch contest finalist arrived. Gwen introduced Madison Johnsen, founder of Lentilix.

"Hi! Can I get you something?" Currant said, falling seamlessly back to her fast-food training. "Would you like some coffee? Tea? A scone?" *Lentilix... that's the vegan menu reader.* "We also have sandwiches. Want a Vegan Falafelcado?"

Madison walked over to the airpots. "Coffee sounds great. Can I get some oat milk?"

"The smaller pitcher there has almond milk."

"There's no oat?"

Currant hid a sigh. "Let me run to the Test Kitchen to check. I'll be right back."

She returned three minutes later with two separate cartons. "We've got rice milk and soy milk. Will one of these work?" She left Madison to decide and walked over to the two newcomers in the corner.

"Hi! Welcome," she said. "I'm Currant Keppler. I work here."

"Alex Lee, creator of St*rlight, asterisk-instead-of-the-A. How are you?" Currant shook his hand.

"And I'm Adeel Siddiq from BlockBox. We were just talking crypto. What's your go-to currency—Ethereum or Bitcoin? Or are you more NFT?"

"Wow, tough," Currant said. "I'd have to think about it. In the meantime, what can I get for you? Coffee, tea? We also have a new line of sandwiches: Kale Cheddar Chutney, Gruyere Bacon, Rye Roast Beef, and Vegan Falafelcado."

Alex opted for a Kale Cheddar Chutney and Adeel asked for a Gruyere Bacon. Currant unwrapped the sandwiches, shoveled them in to the mouth of the oven, and pushed a button.

Madison was hovering by the pastries. "Do you know which of these muffins are Applesauce Date Nut? I checked online and I think that's your only offering that has never been sentient."

Currant pointed out the requested muffins.

"So," Adeel prompted, sidling over. "Now. ETH or BTC?"

The door swung open. *Thank you, Gwen.* Currant excused herself to greet Victoria Okoye, founder of Grounds4Life.

"I think this is everyone, right?" Gwen asked.

"No." Currant said. "We're still waiting on one more."

The oven beeped and she ran back toward it.

"Hey, can I actually get that Gruyere Bacon without the bacon?" Adeel asked.

"Sure," Currant pulled it off, set it on a napkin, and put the sandwich on a plate. She handed it over, and then plated Alex's Kale Cheddar Chutney.

"And Victoria? What can I get you?"

"I'll try this Rye Roast Beef," she said. "And can I have Adeel's bacon?"

"Absolutely." Currant reached for the napkin, but it was empty, a half-dollar-sized grease spot still wicking its way outward.

"Sorry," Madison said, swallowing. "Bacon's my cheat food."

The door opened one last time, and Currant looked up, greasy napkin in one hand and a sandwich shovel in the other. There he was, with his expertly mussed hair and disarming smile, as handsome and as mesmerizing as always.

"This is Luke Kennedy," Gwen said. "From Regulr."

"Currant and I know each other." Luke winked, and Gwen raised an approving eyebrow. "Thanks for walking me back here, Gwen. Have a great afternoon." He turned toward Currant. "Currant Keppler," he said, eyes twinkling. "How've you been?"

Are you kidding me? How've I been? You ghosted me, you asshole. "I'm doing well, Luke. How are you?"

At that moment, Sung-Min walked in. "Hey, everybody. T-minus ten minutes. Grab a coffee or whatever and then head down to the stage so we can get you mic'd up."

Luke looked back at Currant and winked. "See you later, Currant." He walked past the coffee pots, wrinkling his nose, and picked up a bottle of water.

Currant knew she should go down and watch the contest, but she didn't have the energy. *No one will notice if I'm a few minutes late.* She walked idly around the meeting room, gathering plates and napkins off the knife-blade-shaped table, and then wiped down the oven. *I really didn't need that MBA,* she thought. *My fast-food experience and ability to fill in order forms for branded pens have been the only career qualifications I've used so far.*

When Swiss Army Knife was spotless, she walked down the hall and slipped into the last row of seats.

"Next up, our final finalist," Max announced. "Luke Kennedy, founder of Regulr, a startup that couples efficiency and community by providing what we all crave—connection."

Currant stood back up and left.

you in the green room? Sung-Min texted.

yep, Currant replied

pitchers heading back toward you now. not sure how long judges will deliberate – prob at least 30 min – will let you know

Currant sent back a thumbs-up.

The five finalists entered the room, laughing and buzzing from the thrill of the stage. "Another round of sandwiches?" Currant asked. They all shook their heads.

It was only five minutes until Currant's phone vibrated again.

they're done. send em back

"Wow, they've already decided."

"That was quick," said Luke.

With refilled coffee cups and mouths full of scones, the pitch contestants filed back out the door.

"Hey, Luke?" she called as he left the room, voice as artificially sweet as a Salted Caramel Ski Jump. "I really hope you win."

Chapter 32

This time, Currant was full of energy. She marched right to the front row and sat down by Purnima. "I can take over the live-tweeting now," she whispered, and signed into @AlChalCoffeeCo on her phone.

The final announcement took longer than expected. One of the judges was missing; they found him sitting in his car with the AC on, smoking a clove cigarette and recording a podcast. Then Gavin was late, held up in a meeting with the private equity group that held the majority of AlChal's shares.

Purnima leaned toward Currant. "Jenna must be freaking out." She was grinning.

"Yeah, but poor Max."

Max was handling the delay like a pro, channeling his inner motivational speaker to deliver a miniature rousing keynote, but Currant could tell he was struggling.

"Here at Alpine Chalet, we know all about mountains. And sometimes, the path to success can seem like it goes straight up a mountain. Sometimes there are switchbacks. Sometimes the trail is blocked. By a tree. Or a bear. Or a... a... mountain stream." Currant saw panic in his eyes.

"But there's always, without fail, a way to ford that stream," Gavin said, striding through the spotlights and taking the microphone from Max. "You may just have to get your feet wet."

Gavin's aura swept the room, and it filled with light and laughter and applause.

"Thank you, Max, for that inspiring message. You did an amazing job of covering for me, and I appreciate it." He turned to the crowd. "There's no excuse for being late, so I won't make one. But I will apologize. I value your time and your trust, and I'm sorry to have abused them." He placed a hand on his heart.

I forgive you, Currant thought. *We all forgive you.*

Gavin raised the microphone again and began to speak. "Every single one of the young women and men on this stage is an entrepreneur—in the truest sense of the word. 'Entrepreneur' comes from *entreprendre*, French for 'to undertake'. And their undertakings are extraordinary."

He had been facing the audience and now angled toward the pitch contest participants. "You've all taken an idea and breathed it into being. You've all started with a spark and coaxed it into reality. You've all faced mountains, and you've scaled their highest peaks. You have all undertaken—and you have all overcome. One of you, however, has come just a little farther." Gavin grinned at the audience, then grinned at the participants, allowing anticipation to build.

"I am so incredibly honored—*all* of us at AlChal are honored—to recognize *Luke Kennedy*, founder of Regulr, as the winner of Alpine Chalet Coffee Company's Fuel Your Fire Start-Up Pitch Contest!"

Luke stood, acknowledging the applause, and then walked slowly and confidently toward Gavin. The two men shook hands, and Currant snapped a picture for social media.

She checked the result. Gavin's hand was clasped on Luke's shoulder; Luke's perfect white smile was aimed straight at her camera lens. *Wow, that's a great photo. It could go on the cover of Inc.* She deleted it.

The applause died down, and Gavin went on. "Regulr has potential, Luke, and with your energy and drive, I know that you'll grow it into something great. In fact, this isn't even an official part of the prize package, but I spoke with our VP of Business Development, and AlChal would be very interested in harnessing Regulr's power to optimize customer experience. We'll be in touch!" Luke beamed again, genuinely pleased, and Currant took another photo. *Also really good.* She deleted it, too.

"...but let's get back to the official proceedings. Luke, we at Alpine Chalet Coffee Company are so excited to support you and the Regulr team throughout your journey. It is an absolute honor to present you with $10,000 worth of funding to fuel your fire. You'll be able to grow Regulr in a vibrant environment, take advantage of dedicated meeting space, and—of course—energize with amazing coffee and our expanded menu." Gavin reached beneath the podium and withdrew a stack of Alpine Chalet Coffee Company gift cards about eight inches tall, securely tied with a red gingham ribbon.

Sung-Ming caught Currant's eye and grinned. "You can only load $100 per gift card, so we had to give him a lot."

Luke handled it well, relatively speaking. His smile faltered, his eyebrows furrowed, and the hint of a sneer wrenched his lips, but it only lasted for a split-second before his radiant smile returned. It was unattractive and unmistakable, a micro-expression of disgust, and you would have had to have been watching closely to even catch it.

But Currant *had* been watching closely, and her camera *did* catch it. She uploaded the picture to the corporate account, typed **Congrats Luke Kennedy of @Regulr! Winner of Alpine Chalet Coffee Company's #FuelYourFire Pitch Contest #ACCC #FullDayDining**, added a coffee cup emoji and a champagne bottle emoji, and clicked **Tweet**.

The first Like came in almost immediately—from Xander.

Chapter 33

After the contest, when the buzz had died down and Victoria Okoye had been given the green room's coffee grounds, Currant finally returned to her desk. It was after 5:30 on a Friday afternoon, so she expected both of her colleagues to be gone. She was not, however, expecting Beck's cubicle to be cleared out.

She stopped in her tracks, then sank into her chair. *Holy shit*, she thought, taking in the empty work surface, barren except for two paperclips and an ethernet cable. *He's gone.*

She woke up her computer to check her email, and there was confirmation: a message sent to the All-Employees distribution list thanking Beck Baker, CMO, for his contributions to Alpine Chalet Coffee Company, and wishing him the best of luck as he moved on for personal reasons. The time stamp was 4:30 PM.

The next email in her inbox was from 4:31. It was a summons to a meeting with Human Resources on Monday at 8:00 AM.

Nobody likes a troublemaker.

Sung-Min and Purnima were spearheading a Happy Hour to celebrate the Pitch Contest's success, but Currant opted out. "I'd love to, guys, but I think I'm actually just going to head home," she said. "Long week." Sung-Min gave her a knowing nod, and she crossed the parking lot toward the solitude and sanctuary of her Honda.

She got in and found that it was stifling. As she turned on the car and turned the AC all the way up, the events of the last several days roared around her. *I don't want to be around anybody right now,* she thought. *But I also don't want to be alone.* She cleared the office park and saw the highway ramps looming ahead. Instead of crossing the bridge to go east toward home, Currant flipped on her blinker and went north.

Traffic was light and she made good time; as she pulled out of the gas station and waved goodbye to Big Louie, she called her parents and asked them to leave a boat at the Bait Shop dock for her.

"What's going on, sweetie?" Her mom sounded concerned.

"Nothing's going on. Can't a working stiff just decide she needs a weekend at the cabin every once and a while?"

"A working stiff *can*, certainly, but a working stiff usually doesn't..."

"I'm fine, Mom," Currant said, her voice breaking a little. "I'll tell you when I get there."

"Alright, sweetie. We'll run the pontoon over. Drive safe, okay? Love you."

"I will, Mom. See you later. Love you, too."

Currant hung up and tried not to focus on anything but the road.

She pulled into the parking lot at Silent Man Landing about a quarter to midnight. The drive had seemed longer than normal, and her eyes were tired. She turned off the car and sat back in her seat. *Just a few more minutes,* she thought. *Then I'll be home.*

She was just locking her Honda when she heard a car door slam. Currant jumped and turned. A shadowy figure had emerged from a truck and was crunching across the gravel toward her.

"Daddy, I told you just to leave the boat for me!"

He wrapped her in a bear hug, and Currant cried. Everything she had experienced over the past couple of weeks, the dishonesty she had witnessed, the naivety she had felt... the weight of it all became suddenly too much, and she buried her face in her father's shoulder. *I'm not a strong, confident businesswoman,* she thought through her tears. *I'm still just a little girl.* She cried for a long time, her sobs echoing off the treetops, carrying across the water.

Finally, she caught her breath and they headed off down the dock. Moths buzzed under orange sodium lights as they untied the ropes from the pilings and pulled in the bumpers.

"You could have just left the boat for me," she sniffed.

"This pontoon cost more than your MBA," her father said. "You're not driving it alone in the middle of the night."

The next morning, in an Adirondack chair, Currant told her parents everything. About Gianna, about Beck, about the logo and the murder. About the fact that he got fired, about her summons to HR, and about the crimes that had been committed in the name of marketing. She finished speaking, hands wrapped around her Yeti mug, and looked to her parents for guidance.

"It wasn't murder, Currant."

She looked at her mother. "Well, I know I can't *prove* it, but I have the sketch."

"Your boss probably did steal that logo, but he didn't kill anyone. Hold on a second." Janet Keppler went to the kitchen, rummaged through the recycling bin, and came back with the previous day's issue of the Cretin County Gazette.

Deadly Camp Out Café Fire Likely Set By Owner

The fire that killed Paul Manter, 53, of Poppel Township earlier in the week was shown to be arson, most likely set by Manter himself. Poppel-Greenland Volunteer Fire Cooperative Fire Chief Glen Sorenson confirmed the results of the investigation, carried out jointly with specialists from the Minnesota Bureau of Criminal Apprehension, which indicated that a gasoline can was found near Manter's body. The manner of death has been ruled as accidental, however, following the discovery of head injuries consistent with a fall.

On the day of his death, Manter had logged on to his online banking portal and accessed a message indicating he had been denied a business loan for remodeling the

restaurant. Representatives from Thousand Lakes Savings & Loan were unwilling to comment. "It's a terrible loss," said Sig Olafsson, area farmer and long-time Camp Out Café patron. "Paul made the best pancakes in the state."

Beck isn't a murderer. He was unethical and lacked integrity, yes, but he was not an arsonist or a killer. Currant felt a thousand tons lighter as the corporate world went back to being only metaphorically cutthroat. *No matter how high up you get,* she thought, *a job is just a job. You can't take it so seriously. Business isn't life-and-death.*

She looked down at the newspaper and thought about Paul. *Or maybe it is,* she realized. A tear dropped into her coffee.

Chapter 34

After a restorative weekend with her parents, soaking in guidance and support, Currant had come home—on the freeway. Now she was back in the Cities, back on her own, and about to face her future.

She got out of bed, showered, and then took extra time with her makeup. She stood in front of the closet and chose her black skirted suit. It felt somber and funereal, and she paired it with her blood-red kitten heels. *If you're going to go down, you might as well go down looking good.*

The parking lot was deserted when she arrived at the office. She badged her way in, pushing through the doors, conscious that it might be for the last time. Currant walked down the hall, head held high like a *révolutionnaire* on the way to the guillotine, and then sat stoically down in her chair. It was just after 7:00 AM.

"Good morning, Currant."

The voice was soft and designed to be comforting, but Currant jumped. She turned around, Gavin's eyes catching hers before she could even complete the full rotation in her office chair.

"Do you have a minute? I'd like to talk to you."

"Of course," she said, surprised. *If you're going to get fired, you might as well get fired personally by the CEO.* Out of habit, she grabbed her notebook and phone and then followed Gavin down the hall.

"How are you, Currant?"

There was so much sincerity in his voice that Currant wanted to tell him. She wanted to tell him about how it felt to think that someone she worked with was capable of murder, and that, even if not, he was unethical and a cheat. She wanted to tell him that she hated the phrase "Do whatever it takes to succeed", because she had personally witnessed the lengths to which some people took it. She wanted to tell him that she missed the innocence of business school, where her biggest worry was finding enough Journal of Management articles to cite before reaching the monthly pre-paywall limit. She wanted to bring her whole self to Gavin, to be authentic, to open up to him about what she was feeling. Instead, she said, "I'm fine."

Gavin looked over at her, and the empathy in his eyes was tangible. "I understand," he said quietly, and then they were in his office. He motioned Currant toward a molded Danish chair.

Gavin rounded his desk and sank into his seat. Currant perched on the edge of hers. A few beats of silence passed, and then Gavin began to speak.

"Andrea told me everything that happened, Currant, and I wanted to talk to you about it personally. I'm glad we have this opportunity."

Currant nodded and swallowed. "Me too, Gavin."

"I assume you're aware of the latest developments. What Beck did was not a crime, but it obviously goes against everything that

AlChal stands for. We value honesty, integrity, and trust, and these actions flew in the face of all of that. I'm sure you've seen that we let Beck go."

Currant nodded again.

"It's a really tough situation," Gavin continued, "And I'm so, *so* sorry that you're caught up in the middle of it."

Here it comes, she thought. *I'm about to be fired from my first real job for something that's not my fault and that I was trying to fix.* Tears threatened, but she had had practice over the last few weeks, and she managed to hold them at bay.

Gavin leaned forward, locking Currant in his gaze.

"We just really want to put all of this behind us as quickly as possible so that we can keep everyone focused, aligned, and moving forward. You get that, right, Currant?"

"Yes." The thing was, she actually *did* get it. Case study after case study had taught her that an issue like this needed to be dealt with quickly and decisively; strong leaders had to make tough choices that prioritized the good of the organization. *He's amputated the limb;*

now he needs to cauterize the wound. I just wish I wasn't caught up in the cauterization.

"I knew you would understand, Currant." Gavin's eyes held so much compassion, so much pity, that she had to look away.

Her eyes burned more insistently now, and Currant felt small. *I hate corporate life. I hate that no one is real and that people are expendable and that it's just a big cruel game and I don't know how to win.* Tears welled up and blurred her vision. She blinked them back and searched the room, looking for something—anything—to center her. Her eyes traced the collection of coffee mugs mounted along the wall, scanning slowly from one to the next as she fought to focus.

Her gaze settled on the blaze orange mug. *Sam Lake Lodge—that's where the C-Suite fishing trip was.* And there, right next to it, in hunter green: Thousand Lakes Savings & Loan.

The tears disappeared, and Currant saw clearly.

She turned back to face Gavin, sitting straight and leaning toward him. "Been up to Sam Lake lately? I hear it's a great year for walleye. In fact, Beck mentioned the corporate fishing trip... and stopping at a 'backwoodsy place' that you recommended."

His soulful eyes turned to granite.

"And Thousand Lakes Savings & Loan—that's your family's business, right, where you got your start? I hear you're the preferred partner for loans throughout northeastern Minnesota."

She was hoping for fright, or at least signs of shock; all she got was a tightened jaw. *I'll take it.*

"Paul Manter's loan was denied. I mean, I know his death was an accident, but it's still unfortunate. Especially when he had a solid business plan." She paused, heart pounding, and then went in for the kill. "I hope nobody starts... asking questions... about why it was denied."

Currant sat back in the molded chair. She was sweating. *I have no idea what I just did, but I hope I did it right.*

Gavin stared at her and she stared at Gavin. His face was a blank, and she tried as hard as she could to keep hers the same. She clasped her hands to keep them from shaking. Gavin steepled his fingers.

Five seconds passed, then ten. *Don't talk don't talk don't talk,* Currant told herself. She had to outlast him, to force him to break the silence. And, after an eternity, he did.

"Like I said, Currant, we need to stay focused, aligned, and moving forward. How can I best help you to do that? You've been through a lot."

Five minutes later, as Currant walked toward her wing, her phone vibrated. She looked down and saw the subject line of the newly arrived email:

CANCELLED: Currant Keppler - HR, 8:00 AM.

She sat down at her desk and smiled shakily. It was time to get to work.

Chapter 35

They pulled the campfire design out of respect for Paul Manter, and because Legal wasn't sure who else had seen it. Gianna cancelled her vacation plans and revamped the logo, keeping the bold, sharp lines of the mountain and the energizing turquoise and goldenrod palette. She swapped out the campfire for hiking boots, evoking rugged resilience and triumph over adversity, and Currant scrambled to update all of the collateral orders. #FuelYourFire became #FuelYourAscent, and the Full-Day Dining Initiative rolled out on schedule.

Luke worked with AlChal to integrate Regulr into their POS system, although it took extensive IT support. He accepted a buy-out, and then turned his attention to a new idea:

Rgiftr, a distributed platform for gift card liquidation.

After a short external search, Alpine Chalet Coffee Company named Gianna as the CMO, garnering significant positive press. Within a month, she convinced the Executive Committee to drop the college degree requirement for senior positions. She and Currant went to Andy's Bar & Grille to celebrate.

One evening, a few weeks later, Currant settled on to the couch. She had just gotten home from a LATTE Happy Hour—and a stop by Store #4 to see if Toby was working—and wasn't quite ready for bed. She scrolled through her phone and a LinkedIn notification popped up.

It was a message from Beck.

Hi, Currant. Hope you're doing well. I want you to know that I regret using that logo. I apologize that you had to clean up the fall out. Good luck at AlChal and in the rest of your career, and let me know if there's ever anything I can do to help you. -B-

Wow, she thought. *That's class. Offering me career help when he'll probably never be able to find another job himself.*

Hi, Beck, she replied. **Thanks for the note. My time at AlChal hasn't been quite what I expected, but I've learned a lot. Take care, and if there's anything I can do to help YOU, let me know.**

Beck must have been online, because he replied right away.

thanks - will let you know. actually just started a new gig... can't tell you where - alchal's noncompete :D - but loving it so far. take care!

-B-

PS: how'd the bonfire go?

Life returned to normal, more or less. Currant stayed busy, and Labor Day weekend snuck up. She found herself once again on

Keppler Island, surrounded by family, relaxed and at ease.

"How's the job going?" Aunt Kay asked. "Any other major scandals?" A light afternoon rain was falling, so the whole clan was clustered on the screened-in porch, sipping out of plastic stemless wine glasses and can-koozied cans.

"Nope," Currant told her. "It definitely started out a little rough, but things have settled down. We're starting our second rotations soon—I find out next week who I'll be working with for Round Two."

Conversation moved on, and Currant sank into the moment. *The chill in the air, the warmth in the wine... I could stay right here forever.*

But, of course, she didn't. Early the next morning, she was on the road, pondering work and life and balance. The turn-off toward Poppel Township came up, and Currant hesitated. She remembered the tweet that had led her down this road the last time: **Value tradition, but favor growth**. She had grown a lot in the last couple of months; it was time to value tradition.

The lot was empty, overgrown with weeds. The burnt-out building had been demolished, leaving nothing but the pot-holed parking lot and a lonely cement slab that had held the problems and promise of the Camp Out Café. Dandelions marched along cracks in the concrete as Nature reclaimed her ground.

Currant parked where she had parked before, and walked to where the door to the diner had been. She could almost hear the grate of the buzzer, could almost see the worn-down booths. She wandered further, imagining the swinging kitchen doors, and then out toward the back of the lot. *What am I looking for?* she wondered. *Why am I here?*

A spark of color caught her eye; indigo and fuchsia and white. *Wildflowers.* In the back corner of the lot, nestled up against the tree line, someone had left a bouquet. She walked toward the memorial, stopping along the way for a sprig of goldenrod.

As she approached the arrangement, Currant stopped short. The wildflower bouquet was in a sixteen-ounce vase—a double-walled, stainless steel travel mug. She picked it up, turning it slowly, until she found what she knew she would find. There, blazing up at her, with all its crackling, brilliant vitality, was the #FuelYourFire campfire logo.

Currant tucked her sprig of goldenrod into the mug, and then headed back across the lot.

Acknowledgements

This book—like all books—would not exist without the support and encouragement of about a million different people and organizations.

First and foremost, I want to thank my husband. The majority of my motivation for actually putting words down on paper was so that I could read them out loud and hear him laugh, and without his love (sometimes tough), Firebrand would still just be something I'd get around to once I finished all my other To-Dos.

I'm incredibly grateful to everyone who helped me make the final product final: my parents, for sitting me down at the dining room table and going through an early draft page-by-page; Pru Warren, for beta-reading and offering amazing feedback and words of encouragement; Sara Taboada, for eagle-eyed proofreading; Marco Marella, for bringing the cover to life; Tonye Bagshaw, for laying everything out; and Cansin Dalak for engineering the audiobook and enabling me to read out loud to more than just my husband.

Special thanks also to the SBB (which stands for the Swiss Federal Railways, but in German) because the initial draft was written almost exclusively in the train on the way to work. Thanks also to my Shut Up & Write community for keeping me off Twitter and on task by being busily at work in the corner of my screen. Tuesdays at 10:00 AM for the win! And a huge, huge, huge thank you to Dylan Howard, my publicist, for always being in my corner.

Lastly, thank you to all of the amazing colleagues I've gotten to work with over the years. Firebrand takes a campy, loving look at the absurdities of corporate life—because, let's face it, big companies (and medium-sized ones, and start-ups…) can sometimes be ridiculous. But at every single place I've worked, I've met good, kind, funny, effective people.

I'm convinced that the world—even the corporate world—is full of good people, and I'm blessed to be surrounded by so many.

About the Author

Megan Preston Meyer has an MBA and 0.25 of a Ph.D. in Operations Management. She spent more than ten years working in supply chain and analytics; now she focuses on the stories that data doesn't tell.

She's the creator of the *Supply Jane & Fifo Adventures*, picture books that teach kids about operations and supply chain management principles, and the *Corporate Elements Mysteries*, cozy mysteries for millennials that balance life and work.

Megan grew up in Minnesota on the shores of Lake Superior and now lives in Switzerland at the foot of a mountain. She likes to hike, is married, and may or may not have cats. You can find out more about her on Twitter, LinkedIn, Instagram, and on the internet at megan.preston-meyer.com.

Also by Megan Preston Meyer

The Supply Jane & Fifo Adventures

Fifo Saves the Day

Supply Jane Clears the Way

Supply Jane & Fifo Fix the Flow

Find out more at www.supply-jane.com